D1255195

Tales from Grace Chapel Inn®

In Her Sister's Footsteps

Pam Hanson & Barbara Andrews

Guideposts
CARMEL, NEW YORK

To Judy Ward and Joan Andrews,
our sisters and friends for life.

Acknowledgments

All Scripture quotations are taken from
The Holy Bible, New International Version. Copyright © 1973,
1978, 1984 International Bible Society. Used by permission
of Zondervan Bible Publishers.

www.guideposts.org
(800) 431-2344
Guideposts Books & Inspirational Media Division
Series Editors: Regina Hersey and Leo Grant
Cover art by Edgar Jerins
Cover design by Wendy Bass
Interior design by Cindy LaBreacht
Typeset by Nancy Tardi
Printed in the United States of America

Chapter One

"Where's Jane?" Alice Howard looked around the kitchen, her younger sister's domain, then smiled at Louise, her older sister by three years.

"I don't know. I just got in too," said Louise.

"She didn't leave a note," Alice said, "but I guess we can't expect a fifty-year-old to account for every minute of her time. She's not our baby sister anymore."

Louise Howard Smith, widowed and the mother of a grown daughter, nodded, "Old habits die hard, don't they?"

"I guess," Alice admitted, "but it is a bit unusual for her to go off and not leave us a note or something."

"Maybe she's at the chapel."

"No, I stopped there on my way home from the hospital. Rev. Thompson has asked me to notify him when a parishioner is admitted to the hospital, but he wasn't there. I'm sure I would have seen Jane."

"Maybe Jane had some shopping to do," Alice said.

"No, I don't think so. After my last piano lesson, her car was here. She wouldn't do much shopping without it."

"I'm probably looking for a mystery where none exists," Alice said, laughing at herself because she did love reading cozy sleuthing stories.

"Did you check the oven? This morning at breakfast Jane mentioned something about making a chicken-and-noodle casserole for dinner." Louise walked over and opened the stainless steel door even though it was obvious that the oven was cold.

"It's still here in the fridge," Alice said, sounding more troubled when she realized that it was well after six o'clock. "This is strange. Jane takes pride in having meals ready on time. She says it's the hallmark of a professional chef."

"Yes, and I made a point of telling her that I have a church meeting at seven. She was going to start baking the casserole around five."

"Oh dear." Alice brushed back her rusty-brown hair from her forehead but failed to mask her worried frown. "If she isn't back when I've changed out of my uniform, I'll get in the car and drive around town, just to relieve my mind. She could have gone to the hairdressers or to visit with Sylvia."

"The trouble is, most places in Acorn Hill are closed by now," Louise said. "She wouldn't have gone out to eat without letting us know. That's not like Jane."

Louise's short silvery hair, deep blue eyes and pale complexion reflected her calm demeanor, but Alice knew her sister was concerned.

"Not at all like her," said Alice. "You checked our phone messages, didn't you?"

"Yes, as soon as I got back from a trip to the library. I took a room reservation for two weeks from tomorrow, but there were no personal messages."

"Goodness, Grace Chapel Inn is booked solid for the next few weeks. Sometimes I can't believe how successful our bed-and-breakfast has become," Alice said. "When we started, it just seemed like a good way for us to keep our family home and live together."

"Without her expertise as a professional chef, we very

likely might flounder. Can you imagine you and me as gourmet cooks?"

Alice laughed in spite of her concern for Jane's whereabouts. "Oatmeal and boiled eggs aren't the kind of fare that brings in eager guests." She looked at her watch. "I don't think I'll bother to change. You stay here and listen for the phone. I'll drive around and see what I can find out."

As soon as Alice left, Louise's misgiving grew. Jane wouldn't neglect dinner without a compelling reason. Maybe a friend had taken sick, or she'd pitched in to help with an emergency.

Worse, maybe something had happened to her. Louise wasn't given to fearful imaginings, but her uneasiness increased. She'd been so fortunate in her marriage that she'd rarely had to worry about where her dear Eliot was. Once though, freezing rain had made him hours late getting home from the music theory class he was teaching. She'd been so anxious about his safety that she'd paced the house praying for him.

That had been a nasty winter evening. This was May, and it wasn't even dark yet. No doubt Jane would be home soon with an amusing story about how she'd been delayed. Maybe one of the town's residents had invited her to tea and made it difficult to leave. Jane was too kind to rush away if a friend needed to talk. Of course, friends had phones, and Jane was usually conscientious about calling.

Louise went out to the long front porch of their Victorian home, hoping to see Jane's long-legged stride carrying her toward home. Maybe she'd gone for a late afternoon walk, enjoying the spring weather so much that she lost track of time. Unlike Alice, who preferred to walk with her friend Vera whenever possible, Jane usually walked or jogged alone so that she could move at her own brisk pace.

Louise thought of calling several of Jane's friends, but she didn't want her sister to think she was checking on her. Part of the wonderful success the three of them had living and working together was the freedom they gave each other. Each had her own interests. Louise was a musician, spending a good many hours every week giving piano lessons. Alice worked part-time at Potterston Hospital. Besides her profession as a chef, Jane loved art in all its forms and usually had several projects going at once.

The sisters shared a deep and abiding faith in the Lord. Grace Chapel, where their father had served as minister, played a major part in all their lives. In spite of their many different interests, they were united in their beliefs.

Louise now turned to the Lord in prayer, trusting Him to bring Jane home safely.

Louise caught herself pacing the wooden floorboards of the porch and decided to wait inside for the return of her sisters. Perhaps Alice would see Jane walking and give her a lift home.

Time went slowly, and less than half an hour had passed when Alice returned, coming through the back door into the kitchen where Louise was making tea.

"I didn't see any sign of her," Alice said with more than a trace of apprehension in her voice.

"She's probably in someone's house. You know how time flies when women are chatting."

"Yes," Alice agreed without much conviction. "She probably just lost track of time."

Louise didn't believe that any more than Alice did, but they settled down to their cups of Earl Grey tea while they waited. Louise tried hard not to look at her watch or the clock on the kitchen wall, but everything in the room reminded her of Jane. Her younger sister's gift for decorating had made it a pleasant gathering place as well as an efficient work center.

When conversation lagged, Louise caught herself counting

the black and white tiles on the floor. Jane had chosen the room's color scheme, painting the cabinets a warm, rusty red. They'd all agreed to keep the ambiance of the old kitchen with maple butcher block countertops and the old soapstone sink. Even the white curtains with red and black trim and the linen dishtowels were coordinated. Jane worked culinary magic there, which was not surprising since she'd been an outstanding restaurant chef when she lived in San Francisco.

Louise's thoughts were interrupted by the welcome sound of the front door opening. The main entrance was never locked during the day. Jane usually used the back entrance, especially if her shoes were dusty from a walk, but Louise fervently hoped that she'd made an exception today.

Alice was already heading toward the foyer, and Louise nearly spilled the remaining tea in her cup in her haste to follow.

"Sorry I'm so late."

It was Jane, but she wasn't alone. A burly man, muscular rather than fat, held her arm and seemed to be supporting her.

"Have you met Saul Loughry?" Jane asked, limping her way toward the kitchen and lowering herself to a chair with the man's help.

"What happened?" Alice asked, too flustered to acknowledge the stranger.

"I found her along the roadside. She'd fallen and couldn't put any weight on her leg to walk home. I was coming back from a farm where I picked up some plants for my niece."

"Saul is Hope Collins' uncle. He's visiting her from Ohio," Jane explained, stretching her legs with a little murmur of pain. "I met him when I had lunch at the Coffee Shop a few days ago."

"My friends all call me Salty," he said, hovering over Jane as though he expected her to keel over. "U.S. Navy, retired.

I cooked my way around the world a dozen times in my career."

"Nice to meet you," Louise said automatically, distracted by the big tear in Jane's jeans and her disheveled condition. "It looks like you need some first aid."

"Salty rescued me," Jane said with a grimace as her sister bent over her injured leg. "I don't know how long I sat beside the road before he came along."

"I wanted to get back before Hope was through waitressing," the big man explained. "Promised her I'd help plant some flowers in her window boxes. In fact, I'd better get over to the Coffee Shop now that you're in good hands, Janey. She'll think I got lost."

"Well, thanks a lot, Salty," Jane said. "I don't know what I would have done if you hadn't come along. There's not much traffic on that road."

"Glad to help out. Nice meeting you ladies," he said with a nod of his head.

Alice and Louise added their thanks to Jane's, then Alice walked to the front door with him.

"What happened? Are you hurt? Yes, I guess you must be," Louise said bending to look at the ruins of her sister's jeans. "You've skinned your knee pretty badly."

"That's not the worst of it," Jane said as Alice returned to the kitchen. "I have a really sharp pain in my calf. I tried walking back, but my leg kept collapsing on me. It really hurts."

Alice grabbed a pair of kitchen shears and started slitting the leg of the jeans to see what the damage was.

"The first thing to do for a leg injury is R.I.C.E.," she said in a professional tone.

"Rice?" Jane asked.

"Rest, ice, compress and elevate. It's a standard treatment. First I'd better clean away the dirt."

"I'll get our first-aid kit," Louise said, hurrying to fetch it from the storage room.

Alice dampened a cloth and squirted on some liquid soap from beside the sink, carefully washing the blood and dirt from the scrape on Jane's knee, then on the palms of her hands when Jane held them out for inspection. No one talked while Alice expertly cared for the injuries, then taped a large gauze pad over Jane's knee.

"That stings, but it's my calf that really hurts," Jane said, trying to be stoic but obviously in pain.

"How did you take such a bad spill?" Louise asked, unable to hold back her question any longer.

"It was so nice I decided to walk down Village Road to that wooded area east of town. I turned off on Oosterholt Road."

"That's only a gravel road," Alice said. "It gets pretty steep after a half mile or so. Is that where you fell?"

"Not climbing up. I walked in the woods awhile. It was lovely. Wildflowers in bloom, everything so fresh and green. There's a little brook that winds its way through the trees. I could spend a whole day just watching the water ripple over the rocks. I was enjoying myself so much, I lost track of time."

"So you thought you had to hurry home," Alice said knowingly.

"Well, I did plan to put the casserole in the oven at five. Oh dear, you two must be starving. I don't want you to miss your church meeting, Louise. You can warm an individual serving in the microwave. It won't be as good, but it will tide you over."

"Just tell us how you fell," Louise said.

"I didn't realize how soft the shoulder is beside the road. I was going downhill, trying to avoid slipping on the loose gravel, and the ground just gave way under me."

She was clenching her fingers, strands of dark hair that

had escaped from her ponytail brushing against the fair skin of her cheeks. The rust-brown corduroy shirt she'd worn open over a loose-fitting tan T-shirt was soiled from her fall and her chin was streaked with dirt. Louise couldn't help but be reminded of her little sister after a busy day of play among the trees behind their home. Jane had always thrown herself wholeheartedly into the games played by neighborhood children.

"So you fell downhill?" Alice asked.

"Did I ever! Now I know why some people walk with their eyes on the ground. I tried to walk home, but after a few yards the pain got to me. I was resting beside the road when Salty stopped. Thank heavens I'd met him earlier. I don't know whether I would have gotten into a stranger's car, but one thing was certain. I wasn't going to be able to walk all the way home."

"How fortunate that he came along," Louise said. "Alice went looking for you, but neither of us would have thought of going up Oosterholt Road."

"Yes, I'm really grateful to Salty." Jane tried to stand, but she quickly collapsed back on the chair and bent over to clutch her leg.

"We've got to get you to the emergency room," Alice said decisively.

"Maybe if I ice it, then take a hot bath, it will be okay," Jane suggested.

"No, it has to be examined," Alice insisted.

"I'll bring my car around," Louise said. "Then I'll come back in to help you. Stay right here."

In spite of the pain, Jane felt foolish with her leg stretched out on the backseat of Louise's white Cadillac.

She shouldn't have gone so far alone. Her sisters wouldn't have wandered into the woods on their own. Alice was an avid walker, but usually she was accompanied by her friend Vera, a local teacher. Louise liked to walk too, but she tended to stay in town, combining errands with exercise.

"You haven't even had your dinner. I've let you down," Jane said contritely.

"An accident can happen to anyone, anywhere," Louise said in a practical tone.

"I won't feel at ease unless you get that leg X-rayed," Alice added. "If we're lucky, the emergency room won't be too busy on a Wednesday evening."

The drive to Potterston seemed interminable, even though it was a fairly short trip, one Alice made regularly when she was on duty at the hospital. Dusk was falling, but Jane's leg hurt too much for her to enjoy the changing colors of the sky or the warm breeze washing over her from an open window. She loved spring in all its phases, but what she felt now was mostly impatience with herself. She wasn't usually clumsy, and she couldn't remember the last time she'd had a fall. As a kid, skinned knees were her trademark, but she was more than old enough to take reasonable care when she was out walking. Even now, with nothing to do but replay the fall in her mind, she wasn't quite sure what had happened. One minute she was happily making her way down the steep hill, her mind full of the lovely scene in the woods. The next she was dragging herself up from the loose dirt and gravel.

She moved her leg to a slightly different position and winced.

"We're nearly there," Louise said in a comforting voice.

"I think Dr. Harding is on duty," Alice said. "I've worked with him quite a bit. He's young, but he's very good. You'll like him."

Jane wasn't reassured by the prospect of a new doctor. She was going to be uncomfortable, no matter who treated her leg. It would be an ordeal to explain how it had happened, especially since she didn't understand the circumstance herself. Her first reaction had been surprise, but she got a nasty jolt when she staggered to her feet. Something was definitely wrong with her left leg.

Even in the comfort of her sister's car, the pain seemed unrelenting. Alice had given her an ice pack, quickly assembled with leak-proof plastic bags, and tied it on with a linen towel, but the numbing effect wasn't enough to give relief. Her fall and rescue by Salty seemed unreal, but the throbbing in her calf was a painful reminder that it truly had happened.

Louise stopped right beside the emergency room entrance, and Alice insisted on bringing a wheelchair to take her inside. Jane would have preferred to limp along on her own, but there was no arguing with her usually mild-mannered sister on matters medical. Alice had been a nurse too long to have her orders disobeyed. Jane waited and complied with Alice's directions about getting into the chair, but she couldn't help but feel conspicuous as her sister started pushing her into the building.

"I'll park the car and be right in," Louise called through the open window of the Cadillac as Alice hustled her toward the emergency care department.

The waiting area was far busier than they had expected. Alice stopped the wheelchair beside a small reading table and took her place in a short line to check her in. From where Jane was sitting, the process seemed exceedingly slow. It wasn't enough just to show an insurance card. The receptionist in charge asked a seemingly endless string of questions, entering each answer onto her computer with agonizing slowness.

When it was Alice's turn, Jane clearly heard her sister provide enough information to fill an internal revenue form. She nearly expected the woman to ask when Jane had cut her first molars.

A half-dozen other patients were waiting their turns to be

tended to. Most of them ignored the magazines, a rather tattered assortment of health publications, and were only distracted from their own distress by listening to the dialogue at the check-in counter. Jane squirmed as Alice described her fall. Not even her sister's calm, professional manner could mask the fact that she'd been a ninny. How could a supposedly rational middle-aged woman fall down a hill in broad daylight? Jane wanted to dissolve into the chair, be covered over by a cloak of invisibility.

She covertly glanced around the room, wondering what brought so many people to the emergency department on a Wednesday evening. A fair-haired teenage boy presented no mystery. He was holding an ice pack on his wrist while his parents hovered nearby, trying to console him.

"If it is broken," his father said, "there's always next season. You have two more years to play high school baseball."

The boy just hung his head and looked even glummer. Jane easily sympathized with him. When you were that age, a year's wait seemed like forever.

Louise came in from parking the car, and Jane hoped she wouldn't try to comfort her. She was appreciative of her sister's concern, but words just wouldn't help to ease her pain.

As the ice pack numbed her calf, she thought more of the sheer inconvenience of her injury. Would she be able to fix breakfast tomorrow? They had six guests occupying their four guest rooms, and neither of her sisters could prepare the early morning meal. She loved them dearly and appreciated their many talents, but cooking was not one of them.

Alice had lived with their father and cared for him in his final years, but he usually cooked for the two of them almost until the end. In spite of her skilled, caring ways with her patients, she was not as competent in the kitchen. Louise was perhaps more competent, but her idea of meal preparation was heating up some soup or pouring out some cereal. She'd been fortunate that her husband had been something of a gourmet cook and loved working in the kitchen. Louise's fingers were magic on the piano keys, but disaster might beckon if she tried to make anything more complicated than a tuna sandwich.

Jane tried to fill the time by thinking of easy ways to put a good meal on the table tomorrow morning, but she was distracted by Louise's well-intended solicitation and the restlessness of the others waiting to see a doctor. An older woman at the far end of the room looked terribly pale, and a little girl cuddled on her mother's lap whimpered from time to time. The misery in the room made Jane even more unhappy with herself. These people really needed help. She might be delaying aid for someone who was much needier than herself.

"Maybe we should just leave," she suggested to Louise. "We can pick up some aspirin or something at the drug store, and I'll probably be fine in the morning."

Louise looked at her with one brow raised. Alice walked up just in time to hear the sisters' conversation and gave Jane a big-sister frown that squelched her hopes of escape.

Now Jane felt like a rebellious ten-year-old. Her sisters didn't often fall into the motherly roles they'd assumed when she was little, and worse, they were right to insist she be checked by a doctor. Her skinned knee and palms were burning, but they brought more memories of childhood mishaps than serious distress. The pain in her leg was new and strange, demanding attention even though she wanted to ignore it.

Her days never seemed long enough to do everything she wanted to accomplish. Hours flew by so fast that she was always being surprised by the lateness of the day. But not this evening. The waiting room clock was cursed with big bold hands that seemed glued in place. Even when she forced herself not to look, time passed with painful slowness.

"Would you like something to read?" Louise asked, shuffling through the not-very-promising stack of periodicals. "Here's a magazine with recipes."

Jane glanced at her sister's selection and shook her head. The only recipes that interested her at the moment were the ones that wouldn't get made at Grace Chapel Inn if she couldn't cook.

There were still four people ahead of her when the clock had crept up to eight o'clock. Her sisters were both waiting with the patience of guardian angels, feigning interest in magazines that couldn't possibly engage them. Several of Alice's co-workers came up and chatted with Alice, but she kindly didn't elaborate on their reason for being there.

Jane listened for her name to be called as others took their turns. There was an excruciating slowness about the process that allowed far too much time to think about her own injury. The suspense was almost as bad as the pain.

Finally, it was her turn. The pale woman had been waiting for her husband, whose heart pains turned out to be acute indigestion, for which he loudly blamed her venison stew seasoned with chili peppers. The boy with the injured hand came out with his arm in a sling and an expression of sheer misery that had probably had as much to do with missed games as it did with pain.

"Jane Howard," a blond nurse in maroon scrubs called out. "Oh, Alice, I wondered if that was your sister."

Alice pushed the wheelchair, followed by Louise, led by a pert young nurse who chatted with Alice as though Jane were invisible. It was her sister who answered the questions about her condition.

Insisting she could crawl onto the examining table by herself, Jane was outvoted by a virtual avalanche of helping hands. Alice settled her down with a pillow under her head, but Jane sat up, legs outstretched. The feeling of helplessness was more irksome than her reason for being there. She was being swamped by niceness, smothered by concern. The part of her that was grateful was at war with the part that didn't want to be there.

Dr. Ned Harding didn't keep her waiting. He cordially greeted Alice, acknowledged introductions and listened to the information the nurse read from a printed computer sheet.

He was every bit as nice as Alice had said, but she hadn't mentioned that he looked younger than the high school boy who shoveled their front walk in the winter. He was shorter than either sister, thin to the point of looking frail and still suffering from pinkish blemishes that he tried to conceal with a thin fluff of whiskers.

He did Jane one favor. He shooed her sisters away, promising to let them know what was wrong as soon as he knew himself.

Jane didn't know how much time she spent in the emergency room, but she did know that her relief at being released was overshadowed by the diagnosis.

"A torn calf muscle," Louise said as her sisters again went through the awkward process of helping her into the wheelchair. "Poor thing. You must be in terrible pain."

"The compression bandage helps," Jane assured her, "but we have to stop and fill a prescription for pain pills on the way out of town if any place is still open."

"There's one that will be," Alice assured her.

When they reached Louise's car, Alice slid a pair of sturdy metal crutches, on loan from the hospital, onto the floor of the back seat. Jane looked down at them, not quite believing that they would be part of her life for at least the next three weeks.

"The doctor meant what he said," Alice said in her nurse-in-charge tone. "You're grounded. No hopping around trying to do all your jobs one-legged or on crutches. You have to rest your leg and elevate it as much as possible."

"Dr. Harding doesn't run a bed-and-breakfast," Jane said, still trying to imagine how she could possibly lie around for so long.

"You have partners," Louise reminded her.

"You can rely on us to handle everything," Alice assured her.

"I can't do anything for three weeks?" Jane asked, sighing.

"Oh, we'll find things for you to do."

"You've been wanting to read some of the books in Father's library," Alice reminded her.

"We'll work out everything in the morning," Louise said. "Let's get your prescription, then stop for a bite before we head back to Acorn Hill?"

"Good idea, I'm starved," Alice agreed.

After picking up her pills, her health-conscious sisters ordered plump hamburgers and fries and ate them with delight on the drive home. Jane only ordered a soft drink, which she sipped slowly. She thought about how different their lives would be for the next three weeks, and Jane was very, very worried.

Chapter Two

Jane awoke with pain in her leg and sat up groggily. She'd finally fallen asleep on the sturdy cot that Louise and Alice had set up for her in her father's library. She'd agreed with her sisters that it was the best place for her to sleep until she mastered the crutches well enough to climb stairs, but it felt odd to be there in her nightclothes in the bright light of morning.

"Oh no!" she said aloud. "What time is it?"

Her alarm hadn't rung. In fact, it was nowhere in sight. She reached for her watch on the table and couldn't believe her eyes. It was nearly seven-thirty, and the inn had six guests to feed and see on their way. What was Louise thinking, letting her sleep so late? Alice's shift at the hospital began at seven AM today, which meant her oldest sister was trying to prepare breakfast totally on her own.

Groaning, Jane reached for the green silk wrapper that lay neatly folded within reach on an ottoman. Alice had taken away the clothes Jane was wearing the night before, planning to put her ruined jeans in the trash, but she hadn't brought anything for Jane to wear today. There was no help for it. She would have to duck into the kitchen in what she had. She could only hope that no guests would see that their chef was still in pajamas and a robe.

She wiggled into the wrapper but found that tying it securely while sitting was a bit complicated. It flapped open again as she reached for the crutches, remembering Alice's warning not to use her underarms to lean on them.

" 'Use the strength in your arms,' " she said, repeating her sister's instructions. " 'It will be easy once you get used to it.' "

Not at all convinced about the easy part, she pushed herself up on her good leg and wiggled into position on the crutches. That didn't leave two hands free to tie the sash, so she balanced on one foot while she made a good knot that wouldn't come loose.

After maneuvering around to face the closed door leading to the foyer, she took a few practice steps. It felt more like hopping than walking, but she managed some forward locomotion.

"I can do this," she said under her breath.

Now the question was whether she could be of any help in the kitchen. First, though, she sat down again and combed her hair with her fingers, anchoring it into a ponytail using the elastic band she'd taken out before going to sleep the night before. She felt disheveled and in need of a shower, but all the showers were upstairs. For now the urgent priority was to see what was happening—or not happening—in the kitchen.

Even opening a door was a challenge on crutches, and it involved still more maneuvering to get through the doorway. Rather than have a guest see her makeshift bed, she pulled the door firmly shut, using the tip of one crutch as an extension of her arm.

If any guests were still sleeping, the noise she was making was sure to wake them. The crutches thumped on the floor like drumbeats, echoing in the hall. Jane heard voices, but she was too intent on getting into the kitchen to sort them out or to determine where they were coming from.

She started to call Louise's name as she lumbered into

the kitchen, but her jaw dropped and no words came out of her mouth. The kitchen was crowded.

"Here's our wounded dove," a Midwestern voice called out. "Sit down. Bill is making coffee, but I can get you some tea if you prefer it."

"Hettie Fessenden, what are you doing?" Jane asked with astonishment, recognizing the Michigan stamp dealer who stayed with them when she and her husband were traveling to shows in the East. "You're a guest. You shouldn't be working in the kitchen."

"My biggest contribution was putting Bill to work. He's the cook around our place."

"Hettie came down early and saw what a muddle I was in," Louise said, pouring juice into glasses on the kitchen table. "She volunteered to help."

"I volunteered Bill. He has a magic touch with coffee," the petite dark-haired woman said as she arranged folded napkins beside the plates on the table. "Then it just snowballed. All your guests wanted to pitch in and help get breakfast. Wait until you taste the scrambled eggs Mr. Cassidy is making. He adds chives, and Parmesan with chopped tomatoes and just a touch of cayenne."

Al Cassidy was a sales rep who stayed with them when he traveled to eastern Pennsylvania, but Jane had never had a clue that he liked to cook.

"Mrs. Lipton, Dot that is, stirred up some baking powder biscuits. We found some honey in the pantry to serve with them."

"My husband is hopeless in the kitchen, but he unloaded the dishwasher. He'll help tidy up afterward too, won't you, Milt?" Dot said in a teasing voice to her silver-haired, slightly plump husband.

"I'm the one who said we should eat in the kitchen," he said. "No need to be fancy for us."

Their sixth guest held out a bowl of mixed fruit for

Hettie's inspection. "How does this look? Did I cut the pieces small enough?" he asked.

"Perfect, John. Just put it on the table and get the yogurt from the fridge to go with it. Just think," Hettie said enthusiastically, "if we weren't working together, I wouldn't even know Mr. Lowell's name. He's going to North Carolina to visit his parents. They're retired, and he's thinking of moving his software business there to be closer to them."

"Yeah, my dad is a little bored with golf and bridge. He would like to work with me part-time. I think it just may work out." When John Lowell grinned, his long, somber face was almost handsome.

Jane looked around, speechless at all the activity.

"Here, we set a place for you, Jane," Hettie said, pointing to a chair at the head of the table where she would have room to stretch her leg and lean the crutches against a cupboard. "Bill, is the coffee ready yet?"

Her husband, lean, gray-haired and grinning, came over with a steaming glass pot and put it on a hot pad on the table. Others brought the food they'd prepared, and still others brought chairs from the dining room to allow everyone to squeeze in cozily at the kitchen table.

"I believe the Howard ladies like to say a blessing before their meals," Hettie said, "so please bow your heads."

"Dear Lord," Louise said when everyone had settled down, "Bless this food and the good people who helped prepare it. Let their journeys be safe and rewarding, and thank you for the kindness and good will they've brought to us this morning."

Several guests joined in the "Amen," and soon they were all eating and talking as though they were old friends. It was the kind of companionable meal Jane had imagined when they first opened the inn, but she'd always seen herself as the cook. It seemed strange to have the guests in the kitchen, and odder still to be there in her robe. Still, all were enjoying themselves, and even Louise seemed relaxed in her new role presiding over breakfast.

"I'm not quite sure how you hurt yourself," Dot Lipton said. "You fell while you were walking?"

"Think of the nursery rhyme, 'Jack and Jill Went Up the Hill,'" Jane said trying to make light of her fall. "There was no Jack in my mishap, but I definitely tumbled down."

"I know how that feels," John Lowell said. "I did a header on a ski slope once and broke my arm. I couldn't quite believe it was happening until I landed face down in the snow."

All the guests had stories of falls, whether they happened to them or to people they knew. Jane's was quite prosaic compared to the spill Hettie's sister had taken, falling off a bleacher at a Little League game and distracting the spectators' attention from her son's first-ever home run. Her bruises healed, but thirty years later Hettie's nephew remembered the drama of the day.

Jane knew they were telling their own tales to make her feel less embarrassed, and she appreciated it. She was also grateful that no one seemed to notice that she hadn't even brushed her hair properly, let alone changed into day clothes.

"This is our favorite place to stay," Hettie said, "but I don't believe I've ever enjoyed a Grace Chapel Inn breakfast more. Not that Jane isn't a wonderful chef."

"It's just that friendship makes such a good seasoning," Louise said.

Jane added her thanks to those of her sister when the guests started leaving. Hettie and Dot were the last to leave because they insisted on clearing the table and loading the dishwasher. Louise saw them off while Jane sat in weary contemplation at the kitchen table. Jane was immensely grateful that Hettie had organized help for her sister, but they couldn't possibly expect all the guests in the next three weeks to prepare their own breakfasts.

She could hear the sound of the piano coming from the

parlor and knew Louise was taking a music break. Her sister rarely gave in to stress, but when she did feel pressured, a few minutes with Mozart was a great restorative.

It gave Jane a private moment to think of solutions to the breakfast problem. Maybe she could get a stool high enough to let her preside over the stove and counter without having to stand. Of course, there was nothing wrong with her right leg. She could stand on one foot and hop when necessary, maybe using a crutch for balance.

She frowned and tried to think of recipes that would require little movement around the kitchen. There was also the problem of trying to lift things while moving on crutches or balancing on one leg.

"Hello there, Janey," a loud bass voice boomed out from the kitchen door. "I dropped by to see how you're doing. Who's tickling the ivories? Pretty good at it, I'd say."

"Hello, Salty. That's Louise playing. She's very talented. She even has a waiting list of potential students."

"Glad to see you're up and about, Janey. What did the doc have to say?"

"I'll be fine in three weeks or so. Can I get you some coffee?" She automatically asked, not considering how she would get a cup and manage to pour what was left of Bill Fessenden's highly praised brew.

"Thanks, don't mind if I do, but I'll help myself. You don't mind if I warm it in the microwave, do you? I like my java hot as lava."

Jane smiled at the big man's jocularity and nodded approval.

"Putting away lots of strong coffee is a ritual on shipboard," he said, pausing to look at a plate of biscuits left from breakfast.

"Help yourself to a biscuit," Jane invited. "There's butter in the fridge and honey in the cupboard to the left."

She couldn't help noticing the large anchor tattooed on

his bicep just under the sleeve of his black T-shirt. His presence seemed to fill the kitchen, more because of his energy than his height and bulk, although that was substantial. He had a ruddy complexion and wide nose with rather small light blue eyes. His hair was almost too short to identify a color, but it was his take-charge attitude that defined his personality.

"Not bad," he said, sitting across from her and taking a big bite of the biscuit. "I usually use buttermilk myself, but these browned pretty well. Did your sister make them?"

"No, one of our guests." She really didn't want to talk about the breakfast. Now that all the friendly people had left, it felt like a personal failure to have guests making their own meal. "How long are you going to visit Hope?"

"About a month. On June 15th I'll head up to the Soo, that's Sault Ste. Marie, Michigan, where they have the locks. One of my navy buddies has a boat, and a bunch of us vets go on a fishing trip every year."

"That sounds nice. I haven't been to Upper Michigan, but I've heard it's lovely."

"I like to watch the big ore boats on Lake Superior. I heard some take a few passengers. Think I'll look into it while I'm up there. A cruise on the Great Lakes would be a busman's holiday, but I miss being at sea," he said with a chuckle.

"Well, it's nice that you and Hope can have a long visit."

"She's the closest I have to a daughter. Never was on shore leave long enough to get married and have a family of my own."

"Mr. Loughry, I didn't hear you come in," Louise said, walking into the kitchen.

"Please call me Salty," he said. "All my friends do. You're pretty handy on the keyboard."

"Thank you, Salty." Louise said his name, although it sounded a bit strange coming from her. Jane knew she was a person who preferred proper names. "Well, I'm glad you came by. I wanted to thank you again for helping Jane. I wouldn't have thought of looking for her on Oosterholt Road."

"Glad I could help. Say, I wouldn't mind another of those biscuits. They're not half-bad, although, as I was telling Janey, I always use buttermilk in mine." He got up to help himself.

"Louise is a big fan of buttermilk," Jane said, not sure how she felt about being called Janey.

"It's a nice, healthy low-fat drink," her sister said.

"I don't worry much about that," Salty said. "When you're in charge of feeding a shipload of hungry sailors, what counts is volume. Of course, I worked at an officer's club for a couple of years. That was a different story. The brass likes to eat first-class. Took some getting used to, making fancy food. If you ever need gourmet recipes, I'm the man to see. Always made a point of memorizing the popular ones. Saved time when I was under the gun. In the navy, everything has to come off exactly on time."

Salty polished off a third biscuit, then smiled broadly. "Good, but I like to roll them a little bit thicker. Makes the insides moister. Not that these aren't flaky."

As much as Jane appreciated what he'd done for her, he did have rather a strong personality. She felt too tired to continue a conversation with him much longer. In fact, she was longing for a shower and a toothbrush even if it meant scooting up the stairs on her bottom. As soon as he left, she announced her intention to her sister.

Louise was dubious about the wisdom of going up to her third-floor room, suggesting a wash in the downstairs powder room, but Jane was adamant. She was going to master the steps.

Jane started up with Louise hovering behind her, presumably to catch her if she started to fall. Her sister only made Jane nervous. If she did slip, she would probably bowl over Louise and land on top of her at the bottom of the steps. Using a combination of railing, crutch and sisterly advice, Jane inched her way up.

Alone behind the closed door of her room, she experimented with walking on her injured leg. She couldn't possibly do everything that needed to be done while bouncing around on crutches. Cautiously and gingerly, she took one step, careful not to come down hard. Pain shot up her leg like an electrical charge, and she sat abruptly on the edge of her bed.

She was stuck with crutches, at least for a few days. Young Dr. Harding hadn't exaggerated, but she did think that he would inspire more confidence in his patients if he shaved that wispy beard.

After she was clean and dressed in her loosest jeans and a flowing, embroidered top, she felt exhausted. It wouldn't hurt to relax for a few minutes on her own bed.

When she woke up, she was amazed to see that it was midafternoon. For a person who rarely napped, she'd set a personal record for day-time sleeping. Of course, it had taken her forever to get to sleep on the cot. It was satisfactory for sitting and curling up to read but too narrow to allow for much shifting of position. Worse, every time she moved, her leg woke her up. Much as she hated to waste most of the day sleeping, she was probably just making up for a restless night.

The house was quiet, but then, her room on the third floor usually was a silent refuge except for the calls of birds and the movement of trees in the wind. She'd had quite enough of convalescing, though, and it was time to see what was happening downstairs.

Getting to the top of the stairs wasn't difficult, but she stood looking down for several long moments, imagining the movements necessary to propel herself downward on

(

crutches. As was often true in late nineteenth century homes, the polished wooden steps from the third to the second story were fairly steep. If one of the crutches slipped, it could be disastrous.

There was no help for it. It might not be dignified, but she'd have to go down on her bottom. It was better than risking life and limb. She sat gripping both crutches in one hand and using the other to guide herself downward.

Maybe when she got to the wider, shallower steps that led to the main floor, she could risk trying the crutches. She would certainly look silly if a guest arrived when she was descending like a toddler who hasn't quite mastered steps.

When she made it down to the second floor, she positioned herself on crutches at the top of the landing and looked down to the foyer, wishing herself on a level floor. If one good thing came from this experience, it would be a much greater appreciation of what it meant to be handicapped. All those TV ads that showed jolly people riding around on motorized scooters were misleading. It was terribly complicated not to have full mobility. She was lucky that she only had to face a three-week interruption in her usual schedule.

With that thought, she carefully lowered herself to a sitting position and started scooting down.

She was concentrating so hard on getting herself and the crutches down the steps that she didn't realize someone else was in the foyer until she heard the click-clack of high heels.

"Jane, oh dear, can I help you? Here, lean on me."

She looked down at the gray eyes, thinly penciled eyebrows and broad forehead of Florence Simpson, one of Grace Chapel's most active members.

"No, I'm fine," Jane quickly assured her.

She wouldn't have minded a boost to stand and position her crutches, but she couldn't possibly lean on a woman in her late sixties.

"I heard you had a nasty fall," Florence said, "and I rushed right over to see how I can help."

Florence was dressed more appropriately for a garden party than nursing duties. Her watered-silk dress was a pale peach that matched a rather elegant wide-brimmed hat. But then, Florence fancied herself an Acorn Hill socialite, and she was rarely seen out and about in an outfit that wouldn't draw attention.

Jane shouldn't have been surprised that news traveled fast in their town, but she hadn't been expecting condolence calls this soon.

"It was nice of you to come," she said a bit weakly.

"I met several of the ladies from Grace Chapel for lunch at the Coffee Shop. We're the planning committee for the ice cream social. You've probably heard that we're going to raise money to send children to Bible camp. Well, anyway, Hope Collins mentioned to another customer that her uncle had rescued you, and I was quite alarmed. At least you seem to be getting around on your own."

Jane didn't know whether Florence's visit called for sitting in the parlor, but she opted for the kitchen, inviting her to follow along.

"Come have a cup of tea with me, Florence," Jane said. "You can help me by putting on the kettle."

"I have a special tea imported from Scotland. It's what I've been drinking of late. I'll bring you some if you like," Florence said, carefully running water into the tea kettle and holding it at arm's length so no drops fell on her dress.

"We have a pretty good selection, thank you anyway," Jane said, wondering why she suddenly felt weary again.

"Well, as I was going to say," Florence continued as she went about setting cups on the table and finding spearmint teabags that met with her approval, "I know what it's like to be laid up. I don't know what I would have done after my bunion surgery if Ethel hadn't dropped by to help me. I can't tell you how much I appreciated your aunt, not that my Ronald didn't try to be helpful, but you know how men are. He simply doesn't see the things that need to be done around a house, not to mention preparing a decent meal. Of course, if Ethel weren't out of town visiting her son, I'm sure she would have told me about your accident. I wouldn't have had to hear of it at the Coffee Shop."

Jane knew her aunt and Florence had an on-again, off-again friendship based mostly on their love of community gossip. She was glad to hear that she'd been helpful when Florence needed her, but she didn't want her to feel a need to reciprocate.

"I'm sure she was glad to help," Jane said.

"Now, I know your sisters aren't too keen on cooking, so if there's anything I can tell them about running a kitchen, I'll be glad to contribute the benefit of my experience."

Jane was pretty sure her sisters didn't want to be told anything. In fact, Louise had found that working with Florence on numerous church projects had been a bit of a trial. But Jane smiled and accepted the offer in the spirit in which it was made.

"That's very nice of you, Florence. I'll keep it in mind if we run into any problems."

"Have I told you about my cheesy-mushroom breakfast casserole? It's so easy that I'm sure even Alice could make it."

"What could Alice make?" Her sister came into the kitchen in her nurse's uniform, smiling cautiously at having overheard Florence's estimation of her culinary skills.

"Hello, Alice. I was just telling Jane about my breakfast casserole. You must be in terrible trouble now that Jane is laid up. How long do you think you'll have to stay off your leg?" Florence asked, turning back to Jane.

"Three weeks. It will go quickly," Jane said with a decisiveness meant to discourage Florence.

"Oh, that will seem like forever to someone as active as

you are," her visitor said sympathetically. "Well, I really must leave. I have to put a roast in the oven for dinner. Ronald doesn't like his meals to be late. But if there's anything, anything at all, that I can do, you just give me a buzz."

"Thank you for making the tea and for checking on me," Jane said.

"Oh, it's the least I can do. Ethel was so good to me." Florence walked out of the kitchen, and a moment later they heard the front door close

"What did Ethel do for her?" Alice asked.

"I'm not quite sure. She visited after her bunion surgery, but I can't believe that our aunt cleaned house or cooked for Florence. Maybe she fluffed her pillows and listened to the details of the surgery."

"That's more likely. Anyway, I think Florence meant well in dropping by to see you."

"I'm glad you're home," Jane said. "Can you believe I slept away most of the day? Now we need to talk about how we're going to run the inn while I'm on crutches."

"I think you mean, how are Alice and I going to run it?" Louise said coming into the kitchen. "You really must stay off your leg to give it a chance to heal. We need to have a family conference."

"I'm sure we'll find a way to get through your convalescence without letting our guests down," Alice said optimistically.

As much as Jane respected her two sisters' optimism, she prayed for a minor miracle.

Chapter Three

A lice smiled at her sisters as they gathered around the kitchen table for a family conference. It reminded her of the evening when they had bonded together in sorrow over their father's death and had voiced their determination to keep the family home. They had all offered suggestions on how it could be done. It was far too large to maintain just as a residence, especially since Alice was the only one living there at the time.

The decision to open a bed-and-breakfast had been made after much discussion and prayerful contemplation. Alice hadn't wanted to give up her nursing, and Louise had to make the hard choice of leaving the home where she and Eliot had lived in Philadelphia before his death. Even when they had committed themselves, the prospects for running a successful business in their home weren't too rosy. Acorn Hill was a small town some distance from any major city. There wasn't anything resembling a bustling tourist trade, so it still amazed them how many people found their way to the inn.

When Jane decided to join them, their plans began to fall into place. She loved cooking but was ready to give up restaurant work. She'd been weary of night work and the highly competitive nature of her profession. Being in charge of the kitchen at Grace Chapel Inn gave her an outlet for her talent, and her fantastic breakfasts had helped to establish the inn's reputation.

Now they definitely had a problem, albeit a temporary one.

"What we need to do," Alice said thoughtfully, "is find a way to divide our workloads to get through the three weeks it will take Jane to recuperate."

"I heal fast. It might be less than that," Jane said hopefully.

"Or it could be longer." Alice didn't want to be gloomy about it, but her years of experience at the hospital had taught her that healing is an individual thing.

"Oh, don't say that!" Jane protested. "It's only been one day, and I'm champing at the bit."

"We'd better make a list of all the responsibilities around the inn," Louise said. "Then we can see who will do what."

"Hand me that pad of paper by the phone, please," Jane said. "Writing is one thing I can still do."

"Yes, and we can read your handwriting, which is more than I can say for some of the doctors at the hospital," Alice said with a chuckle.

"This is the time of year when I put the most effort into the garden," Jane said.

"I can help there," Alice said. "That's a job that can be done any time during the day. Oh, and I spoke to my supervisor about cutting back on my hours. She promised to do her best, but the nursing staff is really short-handed."

"We couldn't ask you to let the hospital down," Louise quickly said. "We'll work around your shifts the way we always do."

"At least I'm not scheduled to work tomorrow." She was about to make a suggestion when the phone interrupted.

"I'll get it," her sister said, moving quickly to answer. "Grace Chapel Inn, this is Louise."

She listened for several moments, then spoke regretfully.

"I'm very sorry, but we're booked solid this weekend. We would be glad to have you another time."

Louise had no sooner sat down than it rang again.

"I'll get it," Alice offered, catching it on the third ring.

"Aunt Ethel, how nice of you to call. No, Jane isn't in bed. She's right here. Would you like to talk to her?"

She handed over the phone and drew Louise aside for a whispered conversation. She didn't want to exclude Jane from their plans, but they could at least discuss some options while Jane assured their aunt that she was doing well.

Twenty minutes later Jane handed over the phone, and the three of them tried again to do some emergency planning.

"I had one thought," Louise said. "Maybe you can take over my accounting chores, Jane. It's really simple to keep track of income and expenses if you do it every day."

"I want to help, but are you sure you want me keeping the books? Numbers aren't my thing unless they're on a recipe card."

"You'll do fine," Louise said. "I'll teach you everything you need to know."

Jane nodded assent but didn't lose her worried look.

The phone rang again. Alice answered.

"No, Florence, you're not interrupting anything. I'm sure Jane will be happy to have a few words with you."

Ten minutes later Jane ended the call and handed the phone to Louise.

"Florence wanted to tell me about the day she broke her ankle. It still gives her a twinge from time to time."

"I don't remember that," Alice said.

"She was fifteen," Jane said wryly.

"Well, we'd just decided that Jane will do the accounting," Alice said, hoping this was the last interruption for a while. They really did need to make plans for the next few weeks.

"Hello, is anyone there?" a voice called out, punctuated by the little bell they kept on the registration desk in the foyer.

"I'll go," Alice offered. "I wasn't expecting any guests this early, but it will only take a few minutes to check them in and show them to their room. We have couples booked in all four rooms, so we'll have a big group for breakfast."

Hurrying out to the guests, Alice could hear Louise sigh.

"Welcome to Grace Chapel Inn," she said with a smile, approaching the three people standing by the desk with a bit of puzzlement. She was expecting guests to arrive two-by-two, but the couple before her had an elderly lady in an old-fashioned tweed suit with them.

"We're the Wellers," the short, rather stout, middle-aged woman said. "We have a room booked, but I'm afraid we have a bit of a complication."

Her lanky, hollow-cheeked husband let her do the talking.

"We had a caregiver hired to stay with my mother, Mrs. Gilter, while we went to a conference in Philadelphia, but she let us down at the last minute. I'm hoping you have an extra room available for tonight."

"I wish we did," Alice said regretfully, "but we're booked solid."

"I did try the hotel where we're staying for the conference," Mrs. Weller said, "but they couldn't accommodate us tonight. If we don't stay here, I don't know where we'll find rooms." She lowered her voice. "It wouldn't matter if it were just the two of us, but my mother isn't well. Today's trip has exhausted her."

Alice could see that the tiny white-haired lady looked fatigued. The phrase "no room at the inn" came to mind, and she didn't have the heart to send her back to the car in search of overnight lodging.

"Let me speak to my sisters," she said. "Why don't you rest in our parlor. I'll get right back to you." She gestured at the door to the right of the front entrance.

"We have a little problem," Alice said to her sisters in the kitchen. "One of our couples brought an elderly mother with them. I would suggest they go elsewhere, but the older woman is terribly frail. I'm afraid she isn't up to searching for other accommodations for tonight, especially since there are none to be had in Acorn Hill."

"Oh dear," Louise said. "Why did they bring her if she's not up to it?"

"They had no choice. A caregiver let them down."

"What can we do? It wouldn't be fair to give her a room booked by other guests. When we take a reservation, we're promising to hold a place." Louise frowned, her face reflecting the dilemma they were confronting.

"I guess there is one thing we can do," Jane said. "There's my bed. I'm sleeping in the library anyway. I could lend out my room for one night if you really think it's urgent."

"I'm afraid it is."

"We'll have to change the linens and clean the bathroom," Louise said. "Are you sure you don't mind, Jane?"

"It's only for one night, but I'll have to give you a list of things to bring down for me."

Alice was hesitant, but when she offered her sister's bed, Mrs. Weller was immensely grateful. She agreed to let her mother rest in their room until Jane's could be made ready.

Alice ducked into the kitchen to shoo Jane into the library to rest and elevate her leg while she showed the guests to their room, then hurried up to change sheets. Louise gathered supplies to clean the bathroom, but Alice volunteered to finish the job. Louise had two back-to-back piano lessons, and the first child was more likely to be early than late.

"Thank heavens we only serve breakfast to guests," she said as she hurried away to meet her first student of the day.

As soon as Mrs. Gilter was brought to her room, Jane started thinking of things she'd forgotten to ask Alice to bring downstairs. It was irksome not to be able to fetch items for herself, but her real worry was the strain it would put on her sisters to run the inn without her help. Alice had worked a full shift at the hospital, then come home to cope with guest problems and an impromptu cleaning of her room.

Louise's usually calm, dignified demeanor was showing signs of strain too. Jane knew that she liked to relax a bit before beginning lessons, and it was important to her to have individualized plans for each student, but she hadn't had time to prepare today. Fortunately she was working with two beginners, so it wouldn't be as bad as rushing in unprepared when advanced students had their lessons.

Jane had kept the pad of paper and pencil, intending to make a list of her usual duties to discuss with her sisters when they were free, but before she could begin, she heard a familiar voice calling out from the foyer.

"I'm in here," she said, pleased because she recognized the voice of Rev. Kenneth Thompson, their minister at Grace Chapel.

All three sisters counted Rev. Thompson as a friend as well as a spiritual leader. A tall, lean man with dark hair and patrician features, he carried out his duties with dignity, deep concern for the congregation and the community and an inspirational faith.

"Jane, I was sorry to hear about your accident. How are you doing?" he asked, coming into the library through the open doorway.

"It's really not serious," Jane was quick to assure him. "I just need to rest my leg for a little while."

"That's not what Florence told me," he said with a gentle smile that made his eyes sparkle.

Jane smiled weakly, not wanting to discuss Florence's alarmist ways.

"Please, sit down. I'm sorry I can't offer you a cup of tea, but Alice should be down soon. She'll be happy to fix one."

Here she was, depending on Alice for the simplest thing.

"Oh, that's not necessary," Rev. Thompson said. "I can't stay. I only want you to know that if there's anything I can do, don't hesitate to ask."

She couldn't imagine what she might request from a busy man like their minister, but she appreciated his gesture and his pleasant conversation. After a bit, he offered to pray with her for a speedy recovery.

"Loving Father," he prayed, "we ask that You watch over Jane and heal her injury. Comfort her, sustain her and give her patience during her time of confinement. We ask in the name of our Savior, Jesus Christ. Amen."

After he left, she realized why sick calls were such a vital part of a minister's duties. He brought with him a reminder of the Lord's love and concern, but he also showed that he knew her well and empathized with her over the frustration she was experiencing. She sank back on the pillow Alice had put behind her and allowed herself to do nothing but think. By the time her sister returned to check on her, she felt far less fretful.

"I don't think Louise has very high hopes for the little girl who's with her now," Alice said.

"She can't be a worse student than I was," Jane said, confessing her musical ineptitude, even though her sister knew perfectly well that she was tone-deaf and totally lacking in rhythm.

"I had an idea," Alice said, sinking down on an easy chair facing Jane. "Maybe instead of serving breakfast to our guests, we can arrange vouchers for them to eat at the Coffee Shop. They have a good menu, and I've never had a bad meal there."

"I don't know," Jane said. She didn't want to shoot down her sister's suggestion, but it didn't sound like a good idea. Guests expected an outstanding breakfast. The success of Grace Chapel Inn depended on providing one. "Let's talk it over with Louise when she's through with her lessons."

∞

Louise didn't want to admit it to her sisters, but she was frazzled. Nina, her new eight-year-old student, had cried twice during the lesson. Apparently piano instructions were her mother's idea. Louise didn't mind working with children of limited talent, but unless the child was genuinely interested in learning, the result was a recipe for failure. She had to decide whether it would do the child more harm to continue taking lessons or to back out.

Something smelled good, and she followed her nose to the kitchen where Alice had taken the initiative about dinner.

"Pizza's almost done. I found one of Jane's homemade ones in the freezer. I thought we could have supper in the library so Jane can keep her leg elevated."

"Wonderful," Louise said, summoning up a small measure of enthusiasm. "Have most of our guests arrived?"

"They're all checked in. No more problems or special requests. I hated to give Jane's bed away, but I didn't have the heart to send that elderly lady out to hunt for lodging."

"It's only one night. I'll get a tray ready to take into the library. We don't have any buttermilk, do we? I could really use a pick-me-up."

"I'm afraid not. Jane usually does her shopping on Friday. There's no way she'll be doing it tomorrow."

"Yes, we must add that to our list of things to do. And I'll call Justine Gilmore to ask if she would mind doing Jane's room tomorrow as well as the others when she comes to clean."

"I don't mind shopping or doing extra work around the inn, but I'm worried about breakfast." Alice frowned, showing none of her usual sunniness. "I don't have a clue how we'll get along without Jane."

The timer on the stove rang, indicating that the pizza was done.

"Let's eat first, then talk about it. I don't know when I've been so hungry."

Louise was enjoying her second piece of thick-crust pizza smothered in green peppers, mushrooms and Canadian bacon when their conversation returned to the current problems of running the inn.

"I have one suggestion," she said after finishing her last bite. "Maybe we can have breakfast catered."

"That's a possibility," Jane said doubtfully. "Who would do it?"

"We can probably get someone in Potterston. There's a company that caters special events at the hospital from time to time. They did a retirement dinner not long ago, and it was quite nice."

"So many breakfast entrées have to be cooked immediately before serving. I'm not so sure that would work," Jane said. "I wonder if the Coffee Shop could help us."

"I suspect they're too busy with their own customers first thing in the morning," Alice said. "There's one other possibility."

Her sisters looked at her expectantly.

"We could hire a temporary cook."

"I guess if you can find someone willing to work for a couple of weeks, I could supervise," Jane said.

"No, that's not at all what I have in mind," Alice said firmly. "If you're in the kitchen, you'll want to help. Pretty soon you'll be dancing around on crutches. That's not what Dr. Harding meant when he said to rest your leg. We need someone to take over the kitchen."

"You sound as if you have someone in mind," Louise said.

"Hope's cousin, Saul Loughry."

"Yes, he was a navy cook," Louise said thoughtfully. "Didn't he mention working in an officers' club? I imagine he's qualified, but would he be willing?"

"I think that there's a good chance that he would. Hope usually works the breakfast shift at the Coffee Shop. They probably don't have any plans until later in the day. Anyway, there's no harm in asking. He certainly could solve our biggest problem. I can't imagine how we'll manage without some help."

Jane hadn't said a word, Louise noticed. She looked at her younger sister, expecting some comment, but she only shrugged her shoulders.

"You don't mind if we get a temporary replacement, do you?" Louise asked. "No one can prepare a meal as well as you do, but Alice's suggestion is a good one."

"I don't imagine he'll mind being asked. If he says no, we'll consider other options," Alice said.

"What other options are there?" Jane asked.

"None really." Louise laughed. "I'll call him at Hope's and ask him to come by tomorrow to talk over our situation. Meanwhile, what am I going to do about breakfast for our seven guests?"

"I'm not scheduled to work, so I can help," Alice said.

"Let's go over what I have in the freezer," Jane said. "I think we can put together a buffet using all the things I've put aside for a rainy day. And since we have an elderly guest, you can make your specialty, Louise. I'll give you a few hints on how to make your oatmeal seem more interesting."

"Gourmet oatmeal?" Louise rolled her eyes, much to her sisters' amusement.

The next morning Louise awoke with the feeling that she'd hardly slept. She vaguely remembered dreams of being in the kitchen with Alice while guests, dozens of them, clamored for food and banged their forks and spoons on empty tables. In fact, her imagined panic had seemed so vivid that it took a while to shake it off.

This was no time to skip her morning devotions. She

prayed fervently for Jane's full recovery, and her Bible verse for the day gave her needed perspective on the work ahead. She smiled as she read familiar words that had a whole new meaning this morning: "Then the Lord said to Moses, 'I will rain down bread from heaven for you'" (Exodus 16:4).

She wasn't expecting manna from heaven to solve her problem, but she did pray that she wouldn't let down Jane and their guests.

Alice was already in the kitchen when she got there.

"No reason to wake Jane," Alice whispered. "She'll want to help, and before we can stop her, she's likely to try walking on that leg. The more she rests it, the quicker it will heal. I have our work list here."

"What should I do?" Louise glanced at the list Jane had made the previous evening, noticing that Alice had checked off a few items.

"The eggs are ready to scramble, although we're short on mushrooms. No wonder, since this is Jane's day to shop. There's some grated cheese to sprinkle on when they're nearly done. I'll take care of the fruit tray if you want to slice bread. I took it out of the freezer first thing, but it may still be hard in the center."

"How long have you been up?" Louise asked with a twinge of guilt.

"For a while," Alice said evasively. "I woke up and couldn't get back to sleep. I kept thinking of all the things that could go wrong with breakfast. Oh, don't forget your oatmeal. Do you suppose it would be all right to cook it to order in the microwave?"

"It won't be as creamy as Jane's."

"Well, maybe no one will want any. That would solve that problem. Well, not a problem. I just meant—"

"I know what you meant." Louise placed a hand over her heart, feigning hurt. Then she turned her attention to the two loaves of graham bread thawing on the counter. As Alice had predicted, they were still somewhat frozen in the middle. She had to saw hard to get through the icy part.

"It will be awfully time-consuming to warm them individually in the toaster," she said. "Maybe I can spread them out on a cookie sheet and do a whole pan at once under the broiler."

"Sounds good. We only have three oranges left. Should I leave them off the tray?"

"No, section them. I don't think any guests will be upset if we run out. At least we have a nice bunch of green grapes," Louise said.

"I don't really like the way this looks." Alice frowned at the display on Jane's favorite hammered aluminum tray. "There's too much green with the Granny Smith slices and the pear slices. Shouldn't pears be more yellow? I guess I could peel them, but guests could start coming down any time."

"Do as you like, but I don't see anything wrong."

"I guess Jane has raised the bar too high for us," Alice said wistfully, searching for a spoon that wouldn't scratch the pan when she scrambled the eggs.

Louise frowned at the rather ragged pieces of bread on the cutting board and got a stick of butter from the fridge. It was hard getting the butter to spread nicely, and she hoped the delicate brown bread wouldn't burn around the edges before the middles were done.

"Good morning, ladies."

Louise was startled by the booming voice, but quickly regained her composure.

"Mr. Loughry, we didn't expect to see you so early in the day."

"Salty's the name. I might forget to answer to that 'Mister' business. I had my breakfast at the Coffee Shop when Hope started her shift. Thought I might as well drop by. You said something about wanting to offer me a temporary job."

"Well, yes, but I'm afraid we have our hands full right now," Alice said apologetically.

"Say, that's the hard way to butter toast," Salty said, walking over to inspect Louise's efforts. "Just melt the butter and smear it on with a pastry brush. Quicker and more even."

"That's a good idea, but I'm done now."

"Good morning." Jane lumbered into the kitchen on her crutches.

Louise suspected that Salty's booming voice had roused her. Before coming out of the library, she'd pulled on jeans and a pink knit top, brought downstairs for her after she'd relinquished her room to Mrs. Gilter.

"Janey, how're you doin'? I was just telling your sister that it's easier to use a pastry brush to butter bread. Doesn't tear it up like a knife."

"I thawed your applesauce cake and cut it in small pieces," Alice said, again sounding apologetic. "I know it's not really a breakfast item, but some people have a sweet tooth. I was a little worried about not having enough."

"Protein is what people need first thing in the morning," Salty said sagely. "I always made sure my sailors had at least two breakfast meats."

"The covered pan has sausage links," Alice said.

"What can I do to help?" Jane asked, looking around with a practiced eye.

"Nothing at the moment. Alice is going to scramble the eggs as soon as people start coming. I'll serve in the dining room unless someone wants me to make oatmeal. That will only take a minute in the microwave."

"Since I'm here, let me help out," Salty said. "You can't make decent oatmeal in the microwave. I'll make up a pan of a special recipe. I guarantee it will be a hit. I add apples, cinnamon and raisins, then serve it with a sprinkling of brown sugar."

Louise couldn't deny that it sounded better than what she was planning. Salty scrubbed his hands like a surgeon and asked if they had an apron he could use.

"Not that I'm sloppy as a rule," he said. "Just doesn't feel right to be on duty without my apron."

Alice found one for him in a lower drawer. It was bordered with a ruffle and had a pair of bunnies stitched on the front, but Salty didn't seem to mind as he tied it around his muscular frame. Then it was time for everyone to hustle. The guests arrived for breakfast only minutes apart and filled the dining room to capacity. Louise shouldn't have been surprised, given how people usually enjoyed Jane's meals, but she was taken aback by how quickly the food disappeared. Alice scrambled until there wasn't an egg left in the house, and Salty's oatmeal was so popular that he had to make a second batch.

On their way out of the dining room, the Wellers stopped in the kitchen and thanked them again for providing a room for Mrs. Weller's mother.

"Your Christian hospitality has made our trip," Mrs. Weller said. "We can't thank you enough for giving up one of your own rooms."

Alice saw them out, then returned to the kitchen.

"I guess that breakfast went well," she said after the guests had checked out. "Thank you for helping, Salty."

"It was great to man a stove again. Not much challenge in feeding myself, and Hope says she'll get fat if she lets me make too many meals for her."

"About why we asked you here," Louise said. "Jane is supposed to stay off her leg for three weeks. We wondered if you would be willing to cook for us at least part of that time.

We'll pay you, of course, and you would certainly have our gratitude."

"Sorry, I'm not for hire," he said in a somber voice. "The government takes good care of me in return for the thirty years I put in."

"I understand," Louise said with a mix of regret and relief. Perhaps Salty was a bit dynamic for their quiet bed-and-breakfast. They would just have to come up with some other idea. Obviously, she and Alice weren't up to preparing a good breakfast every day.

"Whoa! I didn't say I wouldn't do it. I had in mind a little bartering, I help you and you help me."

"With what?" Alice asked.

"Here's the thing. I heard your pretty music, Lou, and it got me thinking. When I was just a little shaver, we had a player piano. Boy, I loved pumping and listening to the old songs. My great-granddad left us a whole cabinet full of rolls, and I entertained myself for hours playing them. My folks finally decided I could take piano lessons."

"That's nice," Louise said, wondering where this was heading, and whether she appreciated "Lou."

"Well, you know how kids are. I went at it great guns for a couple of years, then I got into sports and stuff. I got so busy my folks made me choose between football and piano lessons. What can I say? All my friends played ball."

"That's a shame," Louise said, sympathetic to anyone who loved music but had to give it up.

"I was thinking about the piano just before I left home in Ohio to come visit Hope. The local veterans have a talent show to raise money for our troops, and I surely would love to play them a song or two just for fun. I remember the basics, but I need some fine tuning, that's for sure."

"You're not too old to take it up again," Alice said.

"I cook for you, and you give me some lessons, Lou."

Louise didn't say anything. She was taken aback by his proposal and wasn't sure what answer to give.

"Louise has a waiting list for new students," Jane said. "It's a wonderful offer, but she might not be able to."

"Oh, just a few minutes every day after I finish up in the kitchen will be fine. I don't want to take up a lot of your time. That is, if you're willing, Lou."

How could she refuse? The man wasn't asking for much, and he wouldn't be depriving one of the children on her waiting list of a chance for lessons. Louise decided to ignore the little warning buzz in her head.

"I think that's a reasonable deal," she said. "But one thing, Salty. My friends call me Louise."

Chapter Four

I've made the grocery list, Salty," Jane said when her sisters had left the kitchen to do other chores. "Maybe you would like to take a look at it. I want to be sure we have everything you might need. Alice will be going to the store for me."

"I always say a good meal starts at the market," he said, taking the list and scanning it. "Oranges, I hope your store has Temple oranges. It's a little late in the season, but you get twice the flavor. I can't stand an anemic orange."

"I'm sure Alice will find the best ones available," Jane said.

"When she buys cauliflower, I hope Al knows to buy the whole head, not those dried out flowerets they sell on a tray. I don't hold with chopping up vegetables and selling them under plastic. I like to take a good look at the produce I buy."

Jane agreed with him, but she was too grateful to her sister for taking over the shopping to be demanding. Anyway, Salty wasn't likely to be using cauliflower for breakfast.

"I've written out a menu for the week so you have something to work from," she said.

"Plan ahead, that's the ticket," he said approvingly. "What's on the docket for breakfast?"

Jane supposed it was only fair to give him input, since he'd be doing the work, but no one had looked at her menus with such a critical eye since she'd graduated as a chef.

"Do you make your own doughnuts?" he asked, even though they didn't appear on her schedule for the week.

"No. Since I can only do three or four at a time in my skillet, they take too long. Our guests tend to want breakfast fairly early. Most of them are on their way to someplace else."

"I hear you. I've done more than my share of getting up at three AM to start cooking. Now that I'm retired, I like to sleep in until five or so."

"I have a stack of crepes in the freezer ready to heat. If they seem too much bother, you can substitute ordinary pancakes."

"Nothing ordinary about my pancakes, Janey. Since I'm only cooking for a few people, no need to dip into the freezer. It's more fun to start from scratch."

"As you like." She could only hope Salty was as good as he sounded.

"I see you have egg substitute on the list," he said frowning. "You don't bake with it, do you?"

"No, but we keep some on hand. We get requests for it from time to time."

"I guess that's okay," he said. "This is a good list, but there are a couple of things I'd like to add if you don't mind."

"What are they?" Jane thought her list was rather complete, but she knew chefs. Each one had specialties, and she had to give Salty the freedom to do things his way.

"Tell you what, why don't I go along to the store with your sister? She can probably use a hand hauling all those groceries anyway."

"I think that would be all right," Jane agreed, hoping Alice wouldn't mind.

"I'll check your pantry and spice cupboard to make sure you're stocked with the things I need."

"I'm pretty sure I am," Jane said, then decided not to make any objections. "But please have a look. You're in charge of breakfast now."

She went back to the library and sank down on the cot gratefully. Everything seemed to be under control. She hated putting more work on her sisters, but all she could do now was follow doctor's orders and get back on two feet as soon as possible.

The problem of breakfast was solved, so why did she have a nagging feeling that she'd already forgotten something?

Alice liked to shop at the General Store in Acorn Hill whenever possible. It was good for the townspeople to support local businesses, but as soon as she saw Jane's list, she knew a trip to Potterston was a necessity. Many of the items simply weren't available in Acorn Hill.

She went into the library to say good-bye to Jane and found her deep in thought, a gourmet cooking magazine lying unread on her lap.

"Is something wrong, Jane?"

"No, not really. I just have the feeling that I've forgotten something."

"I'm sure if it's important, it will come to you. I'm off to shop now."

"Did Salty tell you? He wants to go with you. It sounds like he's quite particular about his ingredients."

"Maybe he just enjoys shopping because in the navy he had to work with whatever they stocked on board ship for him."

"Yes, maybe so. Anyway, I hope you don't mind."

"Not at all. Where is he?"

"He was going to check my supplies. Maybe he's still in the kitchen."

"Well, I'm off. You keep your leg elevated and don't worry about anything."

Alice peeked into the kitchen, then went to the pantry at the end of the room.

"Salty, my sister said you'd like to come grocery shopping with me. I'm going to Potterston, so it will take a couple of hours."

"No problem, Al. I promised Hope I'd take a look at her leaky kitchen faucet today, but I can do it later. It shouldn't take long to replace a washer. Other than that, I'm footloose and fancy-free."

"Well, if you're ready to go, my car is parked on the street in front."

"Better idea. Let's go in my Tracker. Plenty of room for groceries and easy to unload."

Alice couldn't think of an objection, although she really did prefer to drive herself. Before she knew it, she was beside him in his SUV, fastening the seat belt while he started the motor.

His khaki T-shirt and jeans laundered to a pale blue were decidedly casual, but the inside of his car was immaculately clean. He had to be compulsively neat to keep his car as fresh as the day it came off the assembly line. There wasn't a speck of dust on the dash, and the carpeting looked as though it had just been vacuumed.

"Your car is certainly tidy," Alice said.

"I like things shipshape. Maybe I'll stick around the inn awhile after I stow the groceries, clean up a little before I do breakfast tomorrow."

Alice was too surprised to offer any objection. Jane kept the kitchen spotless. Her supplies and cooking utensils were extremely well organized, and clutter was alien to her nature. What on earth did this man plan to do?

When they arrived in Potterston, the supermarket parking

lot wasn't crowded, but Salty found a place in the farthest row where he had several spaces on either side.

"I've had this baby three years and not a scratch on her," he said by way of explanation. "I plan to keep it that way."

The shopping carts were parked outside the entrance, and Alice picked one that was free of flyers, unused coupons and discarded wrappers. She had to admit that it was better to be a bit too neat than to be a litterbug.

She expected Salty to walk with her, but he chose a cart of his own, decided the wheels were listing to the left, then picked another.

"Would you like to divide the list?" she asked. "It would be quicker."

"No, I'll just tag along, If there's anything not on your list, I'll buy it myself."

"That's absolutely not necessary," Alice assured him, mindful that his only payment was a piano lesson. Or maybe more than one. She wasn't sure how many he expected. "If you see anything you need for breakfast, I'll be happy to include it on my tab."

They formed a mini-caravan and moved into the produce department, a rather pleasant setup with a rain forest theme. Soft music played and water misted down on the vegetable section from time to time to keep things fresh. Alice enjoyed wandering through this area. In fact, it was the main reason she picked this store when she shopped in Potterston.

Salty didn't share her enthusiasm.

"Call this asparagus?" he said, picking up a rather pricey bunch of pencil-thin stalks held together by a rubber band.

"It's in season, so it should be tender," Alice said a bit meekly, knowing she was no expert on green groceries.

"Home-grown asparagus should be round and firm. The thickness of the spears has nothing to do with tenderness."

He rejected what was offered there and didn't even seem to notice when the misting system irrigated his arm.

He stopped before a display of green beans being sold by bulk weight and held one up. When he broke it in half, it made a snapping sound that seemed to satisfy him. He scooped several handfuls into a plastic bag and secured it with a wire tie.

Alice couldn't imagine where green beans would fit into a breakfast menu, but she could snap them and cook them up for supper.

"See how white that is," he said, pointing at the rows of celery. "Growers plant them in trenches, then gradually fill them in so the stalks are blanched. Makes for a milder taste, but for cooking I prefer greener celery with stronger flavor, not that you ever find it that way in supermarkets."

He frowned, bunching his forehead into washboard creases, but settled for the celery that was available.

The fruit department pleased him not at all. Alice picked up several large red Delicious apples that would look good on a fruit plate, but Salty quickly nixed her selection.

"No flavor in those," he explained patiently. "In fact, it's darn near impossible to get a decent apple this time of year. I guess Granny Smiths are the best we can do today."

He rejected the bananas as being well past their sale date, and Alice had to agree that some had tiny brown spots that indicated they were overly ripe. She did have her mind set on strawberries, specifically mentioned on Jane's list, but Salty rejected them as "runty little things, not worth cleaning."

After carefully examining every fruit offered and carrying on a one-sided debate about their merits or lack thereof, Salty added papayas, mangoes and nectarines to his cart, carefully double-bagging them and putting them on the collapsible child's seat where other groceries wouldn't bruise them.

Alice gave a sigh of relief that she didn't let him hear. At least the hardest part was over. The packaged goods that they needed shouldn't be so difficult to select.

She soon realized how mistaken she was.

It only took her a minute or two to choose a sealed package of chicken breasts for their Sunday dinner. Jane also had ground beef on the list. Alice found the leanest available and added it to her cart. She was about to pick up an economy-size package of bacon when Salty stopped her.

"You don't want that," he said. "I'll have the butcher slice some to my specifications after he grinds the pork for sausage."

Alice noticed the button that customers could press to summon one of the store's employees. She'd never had occasion to use it, but Salty gave it three sharp jabs, the rings carrying out to where they stood by the long, well-stocked meat case. She felt a bit uncomfortable demanding special service, but the white-coated butcher who came through swinging doors to the rear of the store was friendly.

"What can I do for you folks?" he said.

Salty told him in minute detail.

"I need two pounds of bacon sliced thin but not so you can see through it."

There was a whole section of bacon in the case, thick-sliced, thin-sliced, even artificial protein strips. Alice couldn't imagine what would be different about sliced-to-order bacon, but Salty was specific about what he wanted.

"Then I want two pounds of ground pork for sausage. Trim some but not all of the fat. Use a loin cut. I'd like to see it before you start grinding."

"I'll have to bring it out, sir. Customers aren't allowed in the rear."

"I'll get on with the rest of the shopping," she said, not wanting to be there if the butcher didn't comply with Salty's extended instructions.

Maybe she was being overly sensitive, but she did hate being conspicuous in public. Her sisters teased her that she would let someone run over her foot without a murmur rather than protest.

"Oh, Ally," Salty called after her in a voice that could be heard all the way to the checkout counter. "I noticed Jane is a little low on sage. I'll need it for the sausage. Also I grind my own pepper. Pick some up while you're in the spice section, please."

"Peppercorns and sage," Alice repeated under her breath even though it was highly unlikely that she would forget any order issued by Salty.

She went through her list as quickly as possible, considering that she had to check product dates and brand names as well as the little side notes Jane had written. Nothing was as simple as she would have liked. Even an item like frozen whipped topping, something Jane didn't use very often, came in eight or ten varieties and brands. She didn't want to dawdle and read labels. If Salty caught up with her, he would undoubtedly have some criteria of his own for every purchase.

Her own needs were simple: tissues, cotton balls and shampoo. She hadn't bothered to write them down. As a result, she forgot the shampoo and had to walk back through the store to get it. How long had they been there? It seemed like hours.

She more or less kept track of Salty by the conversations he had along the way. He engaged a delivery man in a discussion of when the stone-ground wheat bread had been baked and quizzed the woman at the deli counter about the ingredients in the broccoli slaw, rejecting it after due consideration. He sent one stock clerk into the back room to see if they had another brand of tarragon vinegar and another clerk to check on whether there were any fresher eggs than those in the cooler.

Did he plan to cook all their meals? Surely Jane had made it clear that his only responsibility was breakfast. It was a relief when he met her at the checkout with his cart only half-full.

On the way home Salty reminisced about meals he'd cooked in the navy. Alice tried to concentrate and make appropriate comments, but her eyelids drooped. She felt as though she'd just worked a double shift in the emergency room and wondered if her schedule for the rest of the day would allow for a little catnap.

"You go on in, Ally," he said when they got back to the inn. "I'll take care of stowing the grub."

She thanked him, wondering why he'd changed his nickname for her from Al to Ally. Every time she heard it, she was hard-pressed to remember that he was talking to her, but it might seem impolite for her to correct him.

Fifteen minutes, that was all she needed to recharge her battery. She thanked him and hurried up to her room, grateful that he was going to put all those groceries away. Shopping with him was like running up a sand dune, but there were some advantages in having a partner to share the work. Today it meant that she could snatch a quick nap.

Jane stared with admiration at the account book open on her lap. Louise's columns of figures were precisely lined up and written in her neat hand. It was a bookkeeping masterpiece, easy to follow and completely legible. Jane hated to ruin the effect by scrawling in the latest entries in her less disciplined writing.

In fact, she'd been dreading the chore, simple as it might seem to her sister. She was sure she would err and put something in the wrong column. It would be a shame to mar the symmetry of Louise's work, especially if she made an error and had to cross out something. Maybe she could pencil in her entries, let Louise check them, then go over them in black ink so they matched the rest.

Or maybe not. That would mean doing the dreaded chore twice. Louise usually used a favorite fountain pen from their father's collection. That meant filling it from the bottle of permanent ink in the desk drawer. Jane much preferred a ballpoint. The job was unpleasant enough without worrying about blotches and spatters.

She even imagined getting her fine-tipped sable brush and painting in the entries the way Chinese calligraphers did. She knew how to handle a brush. She loved to paint.

Keeping the books was the least she could do, considering how much extra work her sisters had. Forget paintbrush and pencil. All she had to do was make a few entries. She resolved to start just as she heard muffled sounds coming from the kitchen. The shoppers must have returned from the market. She could help put things away, if only by telling them where they went.

By the time Jane made it to the kitchen, Alice was nowhere in sight, but Salty had filled the table with bags and was carrying in another load.

"How did it go?" she asked. "Did you find everything you need?"

"Now don't you worry, Janey. I'm on top of this."

"I didn't intend for you to work this late," she said.

"Not a problem. I'll have everything shipshape in time to do a few chores for Hope before supper."

He was sorting out the items that went in the fridge, doing it with a minimum of effort.

"I'll clean the fridge next Thursday when it's not so full," he said.

"You really don't need to do that. I cleaned it Monday. It will be fine until I can do it myself. What's that?"

He hefted a gallon jug that certainly hadn't been on her list.

"I like to clean with this. None of those fancy sprays for me. The old-fashioned products still work best."

"There's room for it in the storage room," she said, concerned about what he might pull out of the sacks next.

"I make my own sausage," he said, taking out a huge tray of ground meat. "I had the butcher grind a good cut of pork. Of course, it's just raw meat until I season it."

"That's nice," Jane said for want of anything else to add.

She couldn't fault his enthusiasm. If he cooked food as well as he talked about it, their guests were in good hands. She didn't want to fall into the morass of envy that some chefs felt toward other skillful cooks. He probably did things very differently, but that didn't mean the results wouldn't be good. She didn't like to be micromanaged herself and shouldn't try to interfere with what he was doing. Still, it was hard when she saw that he'd totally rearranged her perfectly organized spice cupboard and changed the location of her baking supplies. It was going to be a major project to put things back the way she liked them.

"I always consider the guests who've registered before I firm up my breakfast plans," she said. "Sometimes we get children or elderly guests who require a somewhat different menu. And of course, when we have groups of men, I have to allow for bigger appetites."

"Don't you worry, Janey," he said with a booming laugh. "Nobody leaves my table hungry."

"I just thought I'd mention it," she said weakly.

"Now you run along and rest that leg. You can't get better hopping around like a jack rabbit," he said.

She was being shooed out of her own kitchen. She badly wanted to pull rank, but without Salty, the cooking would fall onto her sisters. She left the kitchen, letting her crutches thump out her protest at being evicted from her own kingdom.

☙

Louise checked the foyer for the third time in ten minutes, as though she could hurry along the one guest who hadn't arrived yet. The occupants of the other three rooms had registered in the late afternoon and had gone out to dine or enjoy the tranquility of Acorn Hill on a spring evening.

She frowned at the reservation list. Mr. Bert Frame of Toledo was coming for a long stay but obviously wasn't in any hurry to get to the inn. Rather than be interrupted during her dinner, Louise had insisted Alice and Jane eat without her while she waited for the last guest.

Supper was a simple affair, a big salad and graham bread toast left over from breakfast. She and Alice were too exhausted from all the extra duties to do more than assemble bagged salad greens, shredded cheese, olives and sundry other toppings. Jane agreed that it was a good dinner, given all the other things they'd done that day.

Louise knew she shouldn't be impatient. After all, their guest was coming quite a distance, and a lot of things could hold up a traveler. She occupied herself by making out a list of the jobs that she and Alice needed to do in the next few days. It certainly was a blessing to have a substitute cook, and he'd obviously taken over the kitchen from stem to stern. Her biggest concern was the obligation to give him piano lessons. If he hadn't played at all since he was a child, she had no idea where to start. But like all things, the problem would probably resolve itself in due time.

A loud banging roused her, and she hurried to the front door where a slender man loaded with cases had obviously overlooked the small notice that guests should walk right in.

"Mr. Frame," she said. "We've been expecting you. I'm Louise Smith. My sisters and I run Grace Chapel Inn."

"Nice to meet you, Mrs. Smith." He set down his luggage and shook her hand. "I think I left something in the car. Excuse me just a minute."

Louise stood there among his collection of canvas bags as he scurried out to a metallic blue compact parked on the street. Her first impression was that his car was more color-ful than she would have expected. He was a small man, slim and short with slicked down salt and pepper hair and a tiny mustache that seemed too black for his age. He had pale brown eyes behind round wire glasses and rather prominent ears. His gray business suit seemed a size too large, and his tie was hanging loose, not surprising if he'd driven there all the way from Toledo. What struck her most was his dreamy expression. If a student came to her with that look, she would have expected a poor lesson. She knew when someone wasn't concentrating on the task at hand.

Whatever Mr. Frame was fetching, it seemed to take forever. She looked out to see him rummaging through the car, then stand and look at the vehicle as though he expected it to disgorge the missing item of its own accord. At last he turned, empty-handed, and came back up the path to the inn.

"I was sure I had my cell phone with me," he said in a worried tone. "My wife will be expecting me to call."

"You can use our phone," Louise said. "If you'll just step up to the desk, I can register you."

He left his bags where they were, partly blocking the entrance. Louise thought of saying something, but she hoped that no one would need to skirt around them in the few minutes it took to sign him in.

"I trust that you will enjoy your stay," she said after confirming that he still planned to be there for a long visit.

"Not a pleasure trip," he mumbled. "My company sent me to check on property around Potterston. I can't go into details. Wouldn't want the media to get wind of it until plans are firmed up. I thought it would be more discreet to stay here. This is Acorn Hill, right?"

Louise nodded, a bit surprised that he would ask. Maybe he was only confirming it to himself.

"We serve breakfast starting at seven, but it is helpful if we know approximately when you would like yours."

"Let me think. I have to see a man in Potterston at nine,

but I would like to drive past a property before then. Yes, I think seven would be good. Are you serving dinner now?"

"I'm sorry, sir. We only serve breakfast."

They always made that clear when they took a reservation. She wondered if he'd ever stayed at a bed-and-breakfast before.

"Oh yes, I think I knew that. I suppose there must be some place to get a bite."

"Zachary's is still open. It's close enough to walk." She gave brief directions, wanting to make sure he headed toward town, not away from it. "I'll show you to your room now."

"Thank you. I'll just get my things."

He went over and scooped up several bags, but Louise noticed that he'd left a briefcase behind.

"Would you like me to get that one?" she asked. "The room is upstairs."

"Oh, I did forget one, didn't I? I'll get it."

He set down his larger bag to shove the case under his arm. For a moment Louise thought he would leave the big one behind, and she offered again to help carry something.

"No, no," he insisted. "I have them."

At the door of his room, she handed him a key and reminded him that the fire marshal had prohibited smoking because of the age of the inn.

"Quite all right," he agreed. "That's not my vice."

She left him but some instinct made her turn and look back. The briefcase had again been left behind, sitting outside the closed door. She sighed and knocked, remembering that he hadn't called his wife.

"Oh, I won't need to use your phone," he said after taking the case and thanking her. "I found my cell in my pocket."

She walked down the stairs shaking her head. This guest would forget his head if it wasn't firmly attached. His stay was promising to be interesting indeed.

Chapter Five

Saturday morning Jane woke up before her alarm clock sounded, immediately grateful that she was sleeping in her own bed. Negotiating the stairs was still a chancy business, but she'd mastered the crutches well enough to move about the house without assistance. Unfortunately, the more mobility she had, the more she wanted to help around the inn instead of being confined to the library for most of the day.

She sniffed and realized why she'd awoken. The faint aroma of bacon and maple wafted up to her room. She was as sensitive to smells as she was to taste. Someone was busy fixing breakfast.

Her first instinct was to throw on her clothes and thump downstairs to check on the progress in the kitchen. Instead she took several deep breaths and thought about the situation. Salty was in charge of breakfast, and they were fortunate to have him. She knew how irksome it was to have someone looking over her shoulder while she was cooking. It wouldn't be fair if she tried to second-guess their substitute cook.

Still, she couldn't resist hopping over to her door by balancing on the bedside chair and dresser, then opening it a crack. She could hear guests on the second-floor landing and guessed that they were on their way down to eat. Would Salty's breakfast live up to her standards? Would it be even better than what she would have made?

Over dinner yesterday Alice had told them how particular he was about ingredients. Jane couldn't fault that, although it had been a long shopping trip for her sister.

Jane shut the door quietly but firmly. Much as she wanted to hurry down and see what was happening, she had to trust Salty. He was doing them a tremendous favor. She went about her morning routine, but the urge to check on breakfast grew stronger. At last, when she'd estimated that the guests must be nearly done eating, she couldn't resist any longer. She left her room and began the slow, careful descent to the main floor.

The guests were lingering over coffee in the dining room, and the contented murmurs suggested that they were well-fed. She didn't stop to visit but went right to the kitchen.

"Morning, Janey," Salty called out as she entered. "I hope you're hungry as a bear. There's plenty left, and I'm not one to serve leftovers the next day. I did change the menu. Thought I'd kick off with bacon sandwiches, Salty-style. I spread the bread with a cheese-and-mushroom mix that I invented, add bacon, dip the sandwich in eggs and milk, then sauté in butter. Folks came back for seconds this morning."

"It sounds luscious," she said, wondering why she'd smelled maple.

"I brush a bit of maple syrup on the bacon before I cook it. I like the smell as much as the taste. Get a whiff of that, and your appetite kicks in big-time."

He was tying a black trash bag before taking it outside to the garbage bin. Jane watched him, and suddenly it hit her. She knew what she'd forgotten.

"How could I?" she said aloud.

"What's that?" he said, looking up from his task.

"Oh, nothing. Have you seen my sisters yet this morning?"

"Ally had a bite before she left for the hospital. Said one of the nurses in ICU had the flu, so she had to go in. Lou helped serve breakfast, but I don't know where she's gone. She hasn't had her grub yet."

"Maybe she went back upstairs." The thought of making the trip up to the third floor was daunting, but she urgently needed to see her sister.

"Have a seat. I'll take the trash out, then whip up your Salty special."

"Wait just a bit," she said. "I need to see Louise first."

She made her way out to the foyer, glad that she'd finally gotten the rhythm of moving on crutches. The library was empty, and the guests were still lingering in the dining room, the table only partially cleared. She made her way to the parlor and found Louise sorting through some music.

"Oh, good morning, Jane. Breakfast seemed to go well. I haven't tried Salty's recipe yet, but the guests were enthusiastic."

"Louise, I don't know how I did it, but I've forgotten something important."

"Oh?"

"Remember last winter at the church board meeting when people voted to support the county's clean-highway program?"

"Vaguely," Louise said without looking up from the pile of sheet music. "Didn't they agree that the chapel would be responsible for picking up trash on a stretch of roadway?"

"Yes, a mile between here and Potterston."

"I'm sure it's a very worthwhile project," Louise said absentmindedly. "Are they still going to do it?"

"We are," Jane said unhappily. "That is, the committee that the board formed to get it done. I'm the cochairman."

"Well, there's nothing you can do until your leg heals. Who else is working on it?"

"Several people, but Jack O'Hara is cochair. He's borrowing a truck to haul away the trash we pick up. I don't know how I could have forgotten, but we all agreed to do it in late May or early June. That means any day now, whenever he's able to get a truck."

"Well, you can't pick up trash on crutches," Louise said in a practical voice. "I'm sure people will understand."

"We're committed to do a whole mile. Can you imagine how much debris has accumulated along the road over the winter? I feel terrible, letting the others down. The worst part is that it was my idea. I heard about the program and talked it up. Not everyone thought the chapel should be involved. I had to persuade people that caring for the environment is a way of showing gratitude for the world God has given us. I don't know how I could have forgotten."

"You probably just shoved it to the back of your mind. There hasn't been any mention of it in the church bulletin since last January or February, if I recall correctly. Have you heard anything from Jack about the truck?"

"Not yet. I suppose he could be having trouble finding one that will serve. He couldn't use the animal control truck that he drives on his job. He needs to find one suitable for trash, preferably one with a bed that will tip back to unload at the dump."

"Why don't you give him a call and see whether he's found one? Although I suspect that he'll let you know when he's made the arrangements."

"I suppose so, but a truck is no good unless there are people to pick up the trash."

"I'm sure lots of members will volunteer."

"Jack and I had to be pretty persuasive to get enough people on the committee. We thought of using young people, but the job isn't without risks, working along the highway and picking up who-knows-what."

"It's probably wise to leave it to adults."

"I just feel guilty, putting it all on Jack."

"Goodness, Jack was a marine. I think he'll handle the project just fine."

"My part was to line up helpers. It's hard to ask people to do a dirty job when I can't pitch in myself."

"If it will make you feel better, I'll be glad to help. How hard can it be to clean up along the road? Will we have those sticks with sharp points? That seems an efficient way to gather trash."

"Jack will see to that, but I'm not sure you want to be involved."

"Of course I do. I like the idea of keeping the roadside neat and clean. I would volunteer even if you were able to work yourself. When you talk to Jack, be sure to mention that I'll be on his crew."

"Oh, that's so thoughtful of you, Louise. I still can't believe it slipped my mind."

"Accidents can have that effect. You did take quite a fall, you know. Then you were worried about the inn and the cooking. By the way, have you had breakfast yet?"

"No."

"Then let's have it together. I think Salty is eager to show us what he can do. I wish I felt a bit more optimistic about his piano lessons. It's been a long time since he first learned to play as a child. I wonder how much he's retained, but maybe I'm worrying for nothing. He may have a natural gift .for music."

They started toward the kitchen when a scream stopped them in the foyer.

"It came from upstairs!" Jane cried out.

"Oh, dear Lord, I pray one of the guests hasn't been hurt," Louise said rushing to the stairs.

Salty came from the kitchen and called out, "What was that racket?"

He hurried past Jane and ran up the stairs behind

Louise. Jane followed, moving as fast as she could using one crutch and the banister.

The hysterical screams tapered off to an incoherent babble, and Jane saw their source, a blond, middle-aged woman whose name she couldn't remember.

"I want to leave now," she tearfully told her husband who was hovering beside her on the landing.

"It won't hurt you," he said, trying to comfort her. "It's as scared of you as you are of it."

"It will get in my hair!" She covered her head with her arms. "You bring the bags. I'm going out to the car."

"What's wrong?" Louise tried frantically to get their attention, but the woman ignored her and hurried down the stairs to the front door.

"My wife saw something," her husband said with a helpless shrug. "She thinks it was a bat."

"I saw it too," another of the guests said from the door of his room. "It was definitely a bat. It swooped over the landing, but I don't know where it went."

"We've never had bats, not even in the attic," Louise said with distress. "I don't understand how it could have gotten in."

"Now, folks, there's no danger. Just go about what you were doing. I'll look into it," Salty said calmly, his booming voice reassuring even Jane.

Jane realized that she wasn't going to be much help in the search for a flying menace and made her way back to the main floor. The least she could do was try to soothe the guests and assure them that the inn had never before been visited by bats. She sincerely hoped the word wouldn't spread about a bat crisis.

Louise didn't know how to stop the mass exodus of guests, but at least they had all intended to leave this morning anyway. Their only long-term guest was Bert Frame, and he was nowhere in sight. In their haste to get away, they'd left the bedroom doors open. She followed Salty from room to room, but neither of them saw any sign of the bat.

"I'll check this one too, Lou . . . Louise" he said at the partially open door to the Garden Room, the one occupied by Mr. Frame.

"I'm surprised it's not locked," Louise said. "Most guests secure their doors before they go out for the day. He did come down for breakfast, didn't he?"

"Little guy, looks like he dyes his mustache?" Salty asked as he walked into the room that overlooked the garden on the side of the house.

"Yes," Louise said absentmindedly. She especially liked this room. Jane had given all the rooms a theme when they decorated them, and the garden motif was carried out with varying shades of green. There was a floral border along the wainscoting and at the ceiling, and the elegant rosewood bedroom suite was her favorite among the varying styles in the guest rooms.

Like Salty, she carefully scanned the ceiling and the corners of the room, alert for a startled bat, then watched while he checked the bathroom.

"Not here," he pronounced, "but it's no mystery how it got in."

He walked over to one of the two windows and gestured at the empty space above the upper pane of glass.

"What on earth? All our windows have screens."

Salty picked up the section of screen that normally covered the lower part of the window. For some incomprehensible reason, it was leaning against the wall instead of inserted in the window frame. He adjusted the sash to replace it.

"I'd say your guest wanted fresh air but didn't want it blowing right on him while he slept. He took out the screen, so he could lower the upper section and get his ventilation higher up. That meant an opening with no screen. Don't know why he didn't replace it when he left. Of course, the bat probably came in last night. They are nocturnal."

"We could have a whole colony of bats in the inn," Louise said with a shudder. "We've never had a guest do anything like this before."

"The window is hard to move. Been painted too many times to slide easily, and the damp weather made the wood swell. That could be why he didn't try to close it before he left." Salty grunted from the effort of raising the sash to close the opening. He replaced the screen, shaking his head. "You'll want to have a word with your guest. Pretty careless to go off and leave the window open."

"I certainly will."

"This floor seems to be clear. Do you want me to check the third?"

"Yes, please do." Louise wasn't at all sure what they could do if they did see the bat. She thought of getting a broom or something to shoo it away, but that wouldn't evict it from the house.

She'd left her bedroom door open to get more ventilation, making it the most likely abode of an errant bat. Salty motioned for her to stay in the doorway while he surveyed the room.

"No sign of it here."

They examined Jane's and Alice's rooms, although it seemed unlikely that the bat could gain entry when the doors were closed.

"You never know with bats," Salty said. "They can get through tiny spaces you wouldn't even consider: heating ducts, the space where pipes come through the walls, places even I wouldn't think of looking."

The more they searched, the more worried Louise became.

"All our rooms are booked for the weekend. Should I cancel until we find the bat?"

"Let's have a look in the attic."

Louise crept up the steps behind him, expecting to hear the flapping of wings at any moment.

"It could be up here," Salty said, lowering his voice as though they could sneak up on it.

Louise was so intent on looking at the stairwell above her head that she nearly ran into him.

"The door is cracked," he said, pushing it all the way open.

"Oh dear, it shouldn't be. We rarely come up here. I really should do more checking. I'm afraid we depend on Jane too much. She always has her hands full and then some, just feeding the guests and seeing to their comfort."

Her words sounded hollow in the cavernous silence of the attic. The place was a jumble of castoffs. There were trunks, boxes and discarded furniture, plus things she and Jane had brought from their previous lives and stored there.

"Hard to see up here," Salty said, squinting at the unfinished walls and ceiling.

"Yes, one ceiling bulb doesn't provide enough light to see something as small as a bat."

"I could get a flash, but truth to tell, I don't see much chance of spotting it. There are too many crevices and hidden spots up here."

"I suppose I'll have to call an exterminator. What do you suppose he'll do? Put poisonous gas in the house?" She couldn't help hunching her shoulders in dread.

"Maybe nothing that drastic. Let's hope only the one got in."

Salty went downstairs, but Louise didn't follow until she made sure the attic door was securely closed and all the bedroom doors were shut. She didn't even want to think about the effect the bat had had on one of their guests.

When she was a little girl, her father had trapped a mouse and let it loose outside. She remembered his compassion for the least of God's creatures but didn't know if she could emulate him. She desperately wanted to be rid of the bat. Reason told her it was highly unlikely that the little creature would harm anyone, but its presence made the inn seem unclean. What if it carried rabies? What if it was lurking unseen in one of the bedrooms? Just the fact that it had flown over the landing made her want to scrub down every last inch of the upstairs rooms.

She hurried down to the kitchen, only then remembering that she hadn't had breakfast. Salty started fixing the morning's entrée in the skillet, expecting her to enjoy his first breakfast at the inn. The last thing she wanted was food, but she couldn't disappoint him. Not only was he freeing her from the difficult job of cooking, he'd proved his worth twentyfold by helping her search for the bat.

Jane was at the kitchen table, hearing the details of the bat hunt from Salty.

"I'm going to call an exterminator right away," Louise said.

She found three listed in the phone book, all located in Potterston.

The first didn't handle bats, only insects. The next pest control firm seemed to be out of business. At least, the phone was no longer in service.

"I could make the calls," Jane said. "Your Salty-special bacon sandwich will get cold."

"No, I only have one more to try," Louise said. "Please, start eating without me."

A sympathetic woman answered this time, but, regretfully, they didn't deal with bats either.

"You'll have to call the bat man," she said.

"Who?" Louise thought she was joking.

"I honestly don't remember his name, but everyone calls him the bat man. I have his number. We refer customers to him when they have situations we don't handle. He'll get a raccoon out of a chimney, trap a snake, even help when a bear comes to town and starts upsetting people."

"He catches bats too, I take it."

"Oh, absolutely. He loves bats. That's how he got his name. Here's the number: 555-2669. He may be a little hard to track down. He only hunts critters part time. I think he has another job full time."

Louise thanked her and tried the number. All she got was the answering machine of a man named Duane Van Dinkle. She left a message for him to call her, hoping her tone sounded urgent enough to warrant a quick response.

"I guess that's all I can do now," she said, sinking down gratefully on the chair across from Jane. "I feel as if I've already done a day's work. How do you keep up with every-thing around here?"

"It's a lot easier than sitting around, not able to do anything," Jane assured her.

Salty put a plate in front of Louise, and when she saw the delectable entrée, her appetite returned. She was especially impressed by the way Salty had garnished the plate with very thin orange sections and several dried cherries. Jane always stressed presentation, and Louise complimented Salty on the appearance of her meal.

"It tastes as good as it looks," she said after taking several bites of his breakfast sandwich. "I can tell that our guests are in the hands of a master chef."

Jane added her praise, mentioning that the bread had browned perfectly. "I can taste a faint bit of maple on the bacon. I'll have to remember what a big difference it makes. You've relieved my mind tremendously, knowing that our guests will enjoy wonderful cooking while I'm laid up."

Louise murmured her approval as she finished her serv-ing. "Excellent."

"Tit for tat," he said with a grin. "I can hardly wait for our first piano lesson."

Louise went to the parlor after she finished eating. Salty adamantly refused her offer to help clean up, assuring her that he would make quick work of it and join her at the piano.

She loved the parlor. Not only was it the music room, it was a place of escape that gave her a feeling of tranquility. The wallpaper was embellished with green ivy and tiny lavender violets, and Alice had given her a violet-and-ivory piano shawl for her baby grand. Most of the furnishings were heirlooms, including three Eastlake chairs, an antique mantel clock and two curio cabinets filled with a collection of vases and porcelain dolls.

To pass the time while she waited for Salty, she played a short piece that she'd written herself. At one time she'd had grand dreams of composing an opera. Perhaps one day she would bring together some of her compositions in a longer work.

For now, though, she was content with the work at hand, sharing the duties of running the inn with her sisters and starting young people on the road to musical accomplishments. Some, she knew, would never excel at the piano, and most would probably abandon lessons when life made other demands on them. Still, she hoped that each life she touched would be enriched by a greater appreciation of music.

Salty was at least her age, and she had no idea what to expect from him as a pupil. She'd laid out a beginner's book that might serve for his lessons. Louise hoped he wouldn't think the songs were too juvenile.

Time went quickly when she had a chance to play for her own enjoyment, and her new pupil came into the room before she expected him.

"Do you want the door shut?" he asked.

"Yes, if you don't mind. The room is soundproof that way, although I do tend to leave it open when it's warm and there are no guests about. My sisters never object to hearing the lessons when they're working around the inn."

"I brought my own music," Salty said, taking out a stack of sheet music from an oversized paper bag. "I know you won't be able to turn me into a virtuoso. All I want to do is play some of these World War I songs for my buddies. It will be good to remind them of old-timers who served before us."

Louise started looking through the stack, enjoying the illustrated covers. Some were familiar, and she found herself humming "It's a Long Way to Tipperary," then "Pack Up Your Troubles in Your Old Kit Bag." Others were completely new to her, but she appreciated the sentiments in songs like "The Rose of No Man's Land," in praise of the Red Cross nurse and "Good-Bye, Good Luck, God Bless You."

"I'm not quite sure where to begin," she said, although it did help her to have a narrow focus for the lessons.

"With this one." He pulled a piece of music in a plain paper wrapper from the stack. "My granddad wrote it."

"Let me see," she said taking it from him.

"It was never published. He loved the old tunes and tried his hand at writing a few. He scribbled this one when he was in a trench in France, then made a better copy when he got home. He said it kept his morale up."

"He was in the army then?"

"Yes, the Loughrys were infantry men back to the Civil War. I broke with tradition when I joined the navy. Granddad was in World War I, and Dad was in World War II. He liked to call it the big one. In our town, there used to be a parade once a year honoring the veterans. Granddad and two of his buddies who'd served in France marched as long as they could, then rode on a truck flatbed set up with folding chairs. I remember seeing him, straight-backed and proud in his uniform, when I was still in grade school. The government kept track of how many World War I vets were still alive, and his goal was to be the last one."

"How close did he come?"

"I'm not sure. When my brother didn't come back from

Vietnam, it took the heart out of him. He was gone the next year, and Dad died two years later."

"I'm so sorry."

"Well, I'm the last of the male Loughrys, so I want to play Granddad's song to honor him and Dad and Ted, my brother."

"It's a wonderful way to honor them," Louise said. "Let's see how much work we have to do."

She studied the piece for a minute, relieved that it was relatively simple. In spite of Salty's sorrowful reason for wanting to learn it, she had to smile at the lyrics. She played through the chorus, and Salty sang along in his booming bass.

He's a doughboy from Ohio,
And he'll make the Kaiser quake.
He's a doughboy from Ohio,
And he'll fight for Glory's sake.

"He capitalized Glory because that's what they called the American flag, Old Glory," Salty explained.

"It's very nice," Louise said, responding to his obvious pride in his grandfather. "Maybe you can make some copies so your friends can sing along."

"Good idea. Now, how do we start?"

"Let's see how well you remember some basics."

"Not much, I'm afraid," he said with a chuckle.

"It's a bit like riding a bike. Once you know how, you don't forget." Louise hoped that was true. "Let's start by playing a C minor scale."

She demonstrated by playing it several times, then relinquished the piano bench and took her place in a chair beside him.

He held his fingers over the keys, biting his lower lip in concentration, then started playing. At first she was afraid that he'd completely forgotten everything he'd ever known, but when his thumb crossed under his hand to play an F in the C minor scale, she had higher hopes for him.

"Play it through with your right hand only," she directed.

"Can I play the song now?" Salty asked eagerly after going through the scales with each hand alone, then with both hands together.

"We'll work on a small section at a time."

"You have to learn to crack an egg before you can prepare an omelet," he said philosophically.

Her usual lesson time was thirty minutes for younger children and beginners. Advanced students used a block of forty-five minutes. She'd forgotten to look at her watch when they began, and they'd worked for some while before the time even occurred to her. She was rather startled when she estimated that at least an hour had passed since Salty came into the parlor.

"That's probably enough to absorb for one day," Louise said.

"Do you mind if I practice on my own for a little while? Hope doesn't have a piano, so this will be my only chance."

"Of course not. Use mine any time you like."

She quietly closed the door behind her. If she could give just one-tenth of Salty's enthusiasm to her new pupil, she might make a pianist of Nina.

Jane was in the library, dutifully propping up her leg with a ledger on her lap.

"How are you doing?"

"Fine."

"Have you finished the entries for this week? I can help if you're having trouble."

"No, no, it's my job, at least until I can get back to doing things I like. I certainly have gained a renewed appreciation for your accounting skills. By the way, Duane Van Dinkle called."

Louise stared at her blankly, the name not ringing a bell.

"You know, the bat man."

"Yes, of course. How could I forget the bat man?"

"The good news is that he's coming."

"That's a relief."

"But not until Monday."

"Oh dear, you couldn't persuade him to come sooner?"

"Afraid not, but he said there's absolutely no reason to cancel our reservations. It's extremely unlikely that a guest will see any sign of the bat before Monday. In fact, if it hasn't found a way out, it's almost certainly in the attic."

"I did shut the attic door after we checked there, so maybe it's contained." Louise didn't feel reassured, but she would hate to upset the plans of all the people who would be staying at the inn before Monday.

"How was the lesson?" Jane asked.

"Not at all what I expected. Salty wants to play World War I songs, including a song his grandfather wrote. It will be a memorial to him, his father and the brother he lost in Vietnam."

"So it's not about payment for cooking anymore?"

"No, I really want to help him, even if it means teaching him to play 'Sister Susie's Sewing Shirts for Soldiers.'"

Chapter Six

As a rule, Alice liked Monday mornings. She knew that some people complained about how hard it was to get going on the first workday of the week, but she'd had a varied schedule at the hospital for too many years to feel that way. Instead, she was always refreshed by Sunday services at Grace Chapel and ready for whatever the new week would bring.

She tried to apply her usual optimism to the challenges ahead of her, but little worries nagged at her as she prepared to go downstairs and set the table for breakfast. Particularly she was concerned about her sisters. Jane tried to hide it, but she was fretting about her enforced idleness.

Alice wasn't entirely comfortable with her new status either. It had fallen to her to be the inn's law enforcer, and her first job had been to warn Bert Frame about opening the upper part of his window. He'd been apologetic about letting in the bat but insisted he would get a sinus headache if air blew directly on him. They compromised by moving his bed to a far corner and reversing the head and foot. She didn't enjoy being stern with people, so with luck Mr. Frame would be a model guest for the rest of his stay.

Today she had to deal with the bat man. Would she have to be with him as he hunted for it? She certainly hoped he would find it before Wendell, the inn's gray tabby, could confront it. Bats were notorious for carrying rabies, and she didn't want it anywhere near her beloved cat. Were his rabies shots current? She would have to check—one more thing to do today.

Salty made it plain that he didn't want her to do anything with food preparation, but she felt that the least she should do was set the table and serve the guests. It was true that he tended to call out instructions like the captain of a ship, expecting her to rush each dish to the table the instant it was ready, but Jane had told horror stories of chefs who thought the fate of the world depended on a perfect soufflé. When Salty was head cook on a large navy vessel, he probably had a whole crew of workers at his disposal. He wasn't any more demanding than some doctors she'd worked with, and she could put up with being a sailor subordinate until Jane recovered.

Alice went into the kitchen, but before she could say good morning, she had her marching orders.

"Ally, glad you got here. The first guests should be down in eleven minutes. My special eggs flamenco are nearly ready for the oven. They bake for eight minutes, then have to be served on heated plates. The trick is to serve them really hot, so be sure you use a potholder."

Every dish he made was a Salty special, she noted. Did the man never use a cookbook, or did he make adjustments to every recipe he used? In the skillet she saw a rather interesting mix of potatoes, sausage, tomatoes, pimientos and green spots that turned out to be peas. "I've already set the table," he went on, "but I'll need you to get the tropical fruit cups from the fridge and give one to each guest right away. I don't want them dawdling over the first course when the eggs are ready."

"Aye-aye, sir." If he was going to bark orders at her, she was going to have a little fun with him. He didn't seem to notice.

"The caraway bread is sliced and ready to heat. Don't put out any jam. It only spoils the taste. If someone has to indulge a sweet tooth, they can use a dab of honey."

In her opinion, Mr. Loughry didn't quite understand the concept of "guest." Jane always tried to accommodate different tastes, but Alice reminded herself how lucky they were to have him. It wasn't his fault that he'd spent most of his career cooking for sailors who didn't have much choice about what he decided to feed them.

She did give him credit for unloading all those groceries the other day and putting them away.

Alice didn't even try to have her breakfast until the guests had departed and Salty had gone to the parlor for his piano lesson. She'd politely declined his offer to make the egg dish for her and opted for a bowl of cereal and a piece of toast. Much as she appreciated Jane's gourmet cooking, she was happy with plain fare. Eating alone, she couldn't help remembering how she and Father had often breakfasted together on oatmeal or a bowl of grits with toast.

Her nostalgic mood was shattered by the sound of the phone. She sighed and got up to answer it. "Grace Chapel Inn, Alice speaking."

"Alice, good morning. This is Jack O'Hara."

She smiled, glad that it was a friend instead of another potential guest who would have to be turned away because they were booked solid.

"Jack, how are you?"

"Fit as a fiddle. How are things at the inn? Is Jane getting along all right?"

Of course he would know about Jane's accident. No doubt every member of Grace Chapel knew by now since it was so unusual for her to miss a Sunday service.

"She doesn't like being idle, but I think she'll be fit in a couple of weeks."

"I'll just bet she doesn't like sitting around."

Jack's characteristic good humor was infectious, and Alice smiled. He'd been a good friend for some time, and she could visualize his bright red crew cut and handlebar mustache.

"Would you like to speak with her? She isn't downstairs yet, but I can have her call you back."

"You can give her a message, if you would, please. She probably told you about the highway cleanup. I lined up a truck for this Thursday. It will be harder to get helpers on a working day, but it's the first I could get it. The owner needs it for an out-of-town trip Saturday. Fortunately, my supervisor is a hundred percent for the project and is letting me do it without taking a vacation day. Jane was going to line up workers. Tell her they should meet at the church at nine AM."

"I'll tell her," she promised.

"Fine. I'll get back to her after work tonight."

"Oh, Jack, I wanted to ask you if you know a man named Duane Van Dinkle."

"The bat man," he said with a chuckle. "I send lots of my wild animal business to him. The county only hires me to take care of domesticated animals, livestock and pets. Don't tell me you have a pest."

"A bat. A guest removed a screen and left the window open."

Jack laughed sympathetically. "You have a harder job than I do. Four-footed critters are more cooperative than the two-footed species."

"So we can trust Mr. Van Dinkle to take care of our bat."

"He's the best trapper in the county, if not the whole state. Not only that, but he's the only one I know who's caught an albino raccoon."

"What did he do with it?"

"Oh, they're too rare for euthanasia, even when there's a problem with overpopulation. He let it loose in the woods, although an albino doesn't stand a good chance of surviving:

Without the protective coloration, it's a target for predators such as hawks and owls."

"That's a shame. I would love to see one."

"When an albino is young, I understand that it looks like a cotton ball. They're so rare that I've never seen any myself, but there was a write-up in the Potterston newspaper when Duane caught his."

"Well, I guess we're in good hands. One little bat shouldn't be too much of a challenge for him." She was relieved even though she still couldn't imagine how he would find such a tiny creature in their big house. There were hundreds of possible hiding places.

"That's right. A raccoon is much harder to corner and potentially more dangerous. I've heard of people trying to fend them off with a shovel. The rascals will climb right up the handle and attack. Unfortunately they love living near people. In the woods they live on crayfish and fallen fruit, but in town they have a whole smorgasbord in human garbage. They enjoy the same foods that we do. Not only that, they can get into most garbage bins, and plastic bags don't challenge them."

"How can they open a trash bin?"

"With their paws. They're extremely clever. An old friend had a raccoon declawed and kept it as a pet. Wonderful animal. He would put a peanut in a tin box and hide it. The raccoon would find the box and pry off the lid as easily as a person would. They have a taste for sweets too. I think the bat man uses marshmallows as bait to lure them into his traps."

"Traps?" Alice immediately thought of the cruel snares that maimed an animal.

"Humane traps—cages that close when an animal takes the bait. Duane would never injure any creature if he could avoid it. Don't worry about your bat. Now if you had a raccoon living in your chimney, you would have a serious problem."

"In our chimney?"

"Oh yes. They can climb a sheer wall with their sharp little claws, and they aren't fussy about their domicile. They'll set up housekeeping in an abandoned groundhog hole, the foundation of a building or almost any place where they can curl up. Trouble is, sometimes they get stuck in a chimney and die there. Then the homeowner has a different kind of problem."

"Well, you've made me feel a lot better about our bat," Alice said with a relieved chuckle. "I'll give Jane your message, and I'm sure you'll hear back from her soon. She's really sorry that she can't help with the litter pickup."

"Tell her not to worry. I'm sure folks at the chapel will come through on a project this worthwhile."

Alice hung up, glad that Jack had called. The idea of a bat hunt in Grace Chapel Inn wasn't quite so daunting.

She knew that Louise had volunteered to take Jane's place on the cleaning crew. Ordinarily, she would've been happy to do her share too, but she didn't see how they could both be gone during the day. Fortunately she wasn't scheduled to work at the hospital Thursday, but someone had to be available when new guests arrived. She didn't want Jane to resume that duty yet.

She thought of the things that would have to be rescheduled if Louise worked on the highway. She might be home in time for lessons after school, but Salty's lesson would have to be changed. That was one obligation that no one else could fulfill.

Noontime came and went without the bat man's promised visit. Louise left to do some necessary errands, and Jane was keeping busy by mending a favorite tablecloth that had once belonged to their grandmother. It required delicate hand sewing, and Alice had suggested that she do it as a way to pass time. Jane knew it was make-work, but she soon became interested in trying to repair the antique linen. Alice thanked the Lord that Jane was so good with her hands. Alice gave Jane the news about Jack's phone call and provided some suggestions regarding volunteers.

An hour later Duane Van Dinkle arrived at the back door.

"I came about your bat," he said by way of introduction.

He was tall and very thin with an elongated face and a long nose. Although he was casually dressed in black jeans and a gray flannel shirt, there was a neatness about him that Alice liked. He had a thick cap of jet black hair and a large carefully trimmed mustache, and his eyes were a dark brown that reminded Alice of aged walnut. She noticed his hands too, large and bony with dirty nails. He was carrying a big flashlight and a glass pickle jar with holes punched in the cover.

"Welcome. I'm Alice Howard. We think perhaps it took refuge in the attic," she said. "I'll show you. A guest left a window open, and the bat created quite a stir with other guests when it swooped across the landing."

He made an odd little noise, not quite a grunt. When she tried to make conversation, he narrowed his eyes in a way that made her shiver a bit, reminding her of a Count Dracula she had seen in the movies years before.

"I imagine people tease you about your fondness for bats," she said, feeling uncomfortable with his silence.

"Not when the moon is full."

What on earth did he mean by that?

He followed her through the kitchen and foyer, up to the third floor. When they got to the attic stairs, she indicated that he should go ahead of her. In fact, she didn't have the slightest desire to encounter a flying mammal, but she felt obligated to do what Jane ordinarily would have done.

He moved without making a sound. Alice thought this was probably a good trait for a hunter, but it added to the unease she felt. Most workmen who came to the house were at least a little chatty, but the bat man didn't seem willing to explain what he intended to do.

"Do you see any sign of it?" she asked in a hushed voice that seemed to fit the circumstances.

"Not yet."

He was moving through the attic clutter with great stealth. Although he didn't say so, she suspected that she was a liability to his hunt.

"If you don't mind, I'll go downstairs and let you get on with it. I'll be in the kitchen when you're done."

He nodded assent without turning to face her and continued his intense survey of the attic space.

Apparently concentration was a big part of a trapper's job, and she was disturbing the bat man's. She gratefully hurried downstairs, but her mind was still in the attic with the remarkable visitor.

She wanted to have a brief chat with Jane, but her sister was on the phone in the reception area, trying to line up workers for the highway program. Louise hadn't returned yet, and so far no guests had arrived. It might have been the perfect opportunity to work in the garden, one of Jane's jobs that she'd volunteered to assume. However, it would be better to stay inside under present circumstances. A guest could arrive to register at any time, and the bat man might need something from her.

The kitchen was so orderly that anything she might do there would only upset Salty's system. There were always jobs to be done in the large house, but none that would keep her visible for Mr. Van Dinkle and possible early arrivals. She wasn't used to being so constrained. It must sometimes be irksome for Jane to have to be on constant call for guests, phone reservations, workmen and all the other demands of the inn. If nothing else, Jane's injury had given Alice a lot to think about. She was learning that it wasn't easy to walk in Jane's footsteps.

Should she go back to the attic and check on the trapper's progress? Or maybe Jane would like a cup of tea. She rejected both ideas. At the moment, no one needed her. She was standing watch, just waiting for someone to call on her. It wasn't what she did best.

She went to check the dining room. Everything was just fine. Of course, it would be: Louise had put that room in order earlier. Nothing needed to be done there.

Jane never waited around. Alice couldn't remember her sister ever needing to kill time until her injury forced her to be idle. She woke up with more jobs than most people could possibly handle and sometimes worked well into the night accomplishing everything she wanted to do.

Alice wondered whether she was doing her fair share in running the bed-and-breakfast. She was so busy with her own responsibilities that she'd never really considered how it might be to fill the footsteps of either of her sisters.

"Got it."

She was so deep in thought that the bat man startled her. He walked toward her across the foyer and extended the glass jar, occupied now by a surprisingly small creature.

"I expected it to be bigger."

He grinned and held the captured bat closer for her examination.

"Would you like me to write you a check?" she asked.

"My wife handles billing," he said.

"Well, we really appreciate your catching it. Where was it?"

He shrugged. "In the attic."

"What will you do with it?" It looked so tiny and helpless that she automatically felt protective.

"Release it in the woods."

"Good," she said, realizing that she didn't really want any harm to come to it, but then added, "A far away woods, please."

"Got a rabbit in the truck if you want to see it."

"Yes . . . I'd like that," she said responding to his offbeat invitation.

She followed him out to the road. His vehicle may have started as a pickup truck, but he'd modified it to hold a number of cages sheltered under a roof.

"Gardens don't have a chance with rabbits," he said by way of explanation, putting the jar with the bat in a secure spot between two cages.

"Will you release the rabbit?" she asked, tempted to pick up the small, frightened creature and comfort it.

He made a sound that could be interpreted as yes or no. "Any more problems, let me know. Do you have a guard on your chimney?"

"A guard?" It had never occurred to her.

"A lot of critters can get trapped trying to get in through the chimney. Bats, birds, worst of all, raccoons. Had a mother and two babies die in a chimney north of Potterston. Nasty job, that, trying to get them out after the owner started smelling them."

"I can imagine. What do you mean by a guard?"

"Just a metal grid. Smoke gets out all right, but nothing as big as a bat can get in."

"How would I get one of them?"

Since her talk with Jack, she was easily convinced that raccoons could be big trouble.

"I can put one up for you. Not today. Maybe later in the week."

Alice's first reaction was to talk it over with her sisters. But no, Jane was absorbed in finding trash pickers, and Louise had enough to deal with. She could take responsibility for this decision.

"You know, that sounds like a good idea," she said. "Install one as soon as you get the chance."

He nodded assent and took a small notebook from his shirt pocket, making a brief entry. As he drove away, she realized that she hadn't asked what it would cost. There was a reason why Louise was in charge of finances. If it turned out to be expensive, she would insist on paying for it from her nursing salary.

Louise had offered to cancel her dentist appointment that afternoon, but Alice insisted that she keep it. There was no reason why she couldn't be on call for guests. They had reservations made by a couple who lived in Erie, a sales representative who had stayed there before and a single woman from Chicago.

She was always curious about their guests' reasons for coming to Acorn Hill, although the Howard sisters made it a point not to pry into visitors' affairs. Most, however, volunteered information about themselves. That was certainly true of the Erie couple when they arrived. They were on their way to see a new grandchild in eastern Virginia, but neither liked to fly. Instead they were driving short distances every day and enjoying the sights along the way. A friend had recommended Grace Chapel Inn, and they seemed charmed by the Victorian ambiance.

Alice kept busy dusting and straightening as she waited for the other guests to arrive. She was hoping to walk over to the bookstore and pick up a mystery she'd ordered, but it might not be possible today. As soon as Louise got home, she had students coming for their lessons.

She was in the parlor dusting when a voice called out.

"Hello, is anyone here?"

Alice hurried out to see a slender, rather elegant woman standing beside the registration desk.

"Welcome to Grace Chapel Inn," she said, noticing a matched set of blue luggage. "I'm Alice Howard."

"I'm Emily Cleary."

"Yes, Miss Cleary. We have you booked for a two-week stay."

"I may leave a bit earlier if that won't be a problem. Or perhaps not."

"Either way is fine."

They'd been well booked for so long that an empty room would allow for some spring housecleaning. In fact, they'd rarely been busier, and a vacant room would likely fill up on short notice.

"Did you have any trouble finding us?" Alice asked as she processed a credit card.

"No, in fact, I'm familiar with the area. I went to Penn State. I'm actually here to see a friend who lives in Potterston. He recommended your bed-and-breakfast."

"I'm delighted that he did. I hope you enjoy your visit."

Alice led the way to the Sunset Room at the front of the house, one of two guest rooms with a private bath. It struck her that this was a good choice for Emily Cleary. It had creamy antiqued furniture and Impressionist prints, including one that seemed to harmonize with the way the woman presented herself. It had delicate flowers against a soft blue sky in a shade not unlike the blouse Miss Cleary was wearing. Her pantsuit was blue too, and she'd pulled off the difficult trick of harmonizing two different blues in her outfit. Although she was certainly well dressed, it was the soft, somewhat dreamy beauty of her lined face that was most striking. It radiated kindness, a trait that no amount of artifice could produce.

"Your blouse is a lovely shade," Alice said.

"Oh, thank you. I'm afraid my friends get tired of seeing me in blue. I love it and wear it all the time."

"It certainly suits you. Is there anything else I can do for you?"

"No, I'm fine. This room is lovely, especially the prints. I travel a lot and get tired of motel art. I would rather see a reproduction of a really great painting like that one by Van Gogh than a piece selected to match the bedspread."

Alice laughed, sorry that Jane wasn't there to talk about art with their new guest. She didn't pretend to know as much about art as did her younger sister, and she deferred to Jane's taste when it came to decorating the inn. She wondered what the décor would be if Jane hadn't used her considerable talents.

"We start serving breakfast at seven. You can come any time, but most guests prefer to let us know when they would like to eat. If they're traveling, it speeds things up."

"I think I'll be a lazybones and not come down until eight o'clock," she said with a pleasantly light laugh.

"If there's nothing else I can tell you, Miss Cleary, I hope you enjoy your stay."

"Oh, please call me Emily. And I'll call you Alice, if you don't mind. Actually, I'm much too nervous to enjoy anything at the moment. I'm afraid this is a life-changing trip for me."

"I hope you're not here because of some misfortune."

"No, nothing like that. In fact, it could have a marvelous outcome if I can only make up my mind whether I want to be married."

"Oh." Alice didn't know how to respond without seeming to pry.

"I know I'm well beyond the blushing-bride years. I've been single my whole life, and I never dreamed of marrying at my age."

"You're not too old." Alice certainly didn't think of herself as elderly, and Emily could be as much as ten years younger.

"That's what Henry keeps telling me. He lives in Potterston and has for most of his life. In fact, he's never thought of living anywhere else. He has a business there and is deeply rooted in the community. His father and grandfather were the town's locksmiths, and now he is. He also installs and services security systems, so he's pretty much tied to his work."

"That's an important contribution to the town. I work at the hospital there as a nurse. Naturally I'm biased in favor of Acorn Hill, but Potterston has a lot to offer."

"Oh, I'm sure that's true. It's just that I'm very committed to my work, and it involves a lot of travel. I can be in Senegal one week and Guatemala the next. I don't know if I'm capable of living a settled life in a small town, especially if it means giving up my profession."

"What do you do?"

"I work for an organization that provides dental care in desperately poor areas. Dentists volunteer their time, usually for two-week periods. We have some who come back year after year, using their vacation time to help others."

"Are you a dentist?"

"No, my job is to help set up the clinics. We work with other aid organizations to target the most impoverished areas. There's fundraising involved, of course, and I work with companies that donate supplies. Chicago is my home base, but sometimes it seems that I spend more time on airplanes than in my apartment."

"I know about doctors who volunteer abroad, but this is the first I've heard of dentists."

"Believe me, there's an urgent need for good dental care. Our dentists treat children who've never seen a toothbrush. Some compare what they do to battlefield work. They try to help the most severe cases, but there's never enough time for everyone who needs help."

"I can see where it would be extremely difficult to give up your job," Alice said.

"I'm not young, and the idea of spending my retirement years with a man I admire and love is so tempting. But I don't know if I'm ready to make that commitment yet. Oh dear, here we've just met and I've burdened you with my concerns."

"Sometimes it helps to clarify a situation if you can talk to a stranger," Alice said sympathetically.

"You're very kind, but I don't want to monopolize your time." Emily's smile reached her eyes. "Perhaps we can visit when you have the odd moment."

"I'll look forward to it. I would love to hear more about your dental-aid program."

Alice was in a pensive mood when she left their new guest. Years ago as a college student, she thought she might marry Mark Graves. They were very much in love, but neither felt able to change for the other. Her faith was paramount in her life, but at the time it wasn't in Mark's life. She very much wanted to be a nurse, but his life as a large-animal vet required traveling the world to study and treat wild creatures. They parted because they couldn't reconcile their goals in life.

Now they'd renewed their friendship, but there were still obstacles in their relationship. Thankfully, Mark had accepted the Lord, but he wasn't ready to retire from his job as head vet at the Philadelphia zoo and live in a sleepy community like Acorn Hill. Alice was committed to helping her sisters with Grace Chapel Inn and continuing her duties at the hospital. How different would her life have been if she had married Mark and abandoned her training as a nurse?

It seemed that Emily Cleary was being given a second chance to follow a different path. What would she decide? Even though they'd just met, Alice empathized with her.

Chapter Seven

Jane awoke at her usual early hour on Tuesday. She liked getting out of bed to start breakfast before anyone else was up, and her mental alarm hadn't shut down while she was sidelined. Even though she didn't have her usual reason to go downstairs, she showered and dressed for the day.

It had been nearly a week since her fall, and she gingerly tested her leg to see if she could walk on it. The pain had lessened considerably, but there was still no way she could abandon the crutches. Like it or not, she was going to have to follow doctor's directions a little while longer.

That didn't mean she couldn't pop into the kitchen to see what Salty was fixing. Maybe she could do an odd job, something to keep her hands busy.

In spite of the laborious process of descending the steps, she got down well ahead of any guests, curious to see what was on the menu. Their substitute cook had scrapped most of her suggestions, but she understood. It was much more fun to come up with original meal plans. She couldn't complain if he wanted the satisfaction of making his own favorite entrées.

She thumped her crutches in the foyer to warn him of her coming. It wasn't her intention to sneak up on him.

"Good morning, Salty," she said as she went through the doorway.

"Mornin', Janey. Have a seat, and I'll get your breakfast in a few minutes. I told Ally to sleep in. No reason she needs to help. It's child's play for me to feed your few guests. Even when I worked at the officers' club, I might cook forty or fifty dinners in an evening."

He didn't stop working to talk, and Jane tried to figure out what he was making from the array of ingredients sitting on the counter. A pile of raw apple slices was resting on a cutting board.

"You're making apple rings?" She'd made them to go with ham or pork but never for breakfast.

"Yeah, but not the standard kind. Got to think outside the box, Janey. My Salty-special rings have a pinch of ginger along with cinnamon and brown sugar. I could only find the light colored sugar in your pantry. Usually I use the darker kind, so I put it on the order list for next week."

She'd planned to make the list herself, but it made sense that he would jot down items he might need. She was hoping to go shopping with Alice the next time she went, even if it meant walking through the supermarket on crutches.

When he didn't reveal his entire plan for breakfast, she finally asked, "What else are you serving this morning?"

"Cheese soufflé with mushroom sauce and ground ham patties. I mix finely crushed graham crackers and my special seasonings in the meat."

There was that word again. Everything he made was "special." Jane owned a huge collection of cookbooks and knew that being completely original was almost impossible, but apparently that didn't affect Salty's pride in his own creativity. "There must be something I can do?" She didn't want to beg for a job, but it was frustrating to look on while another chef, however competent, took over her kitchen.

"You can handle the toast if you like. I thought I'd slice this French bread thin, brush on olive oil and brown it under the broiler."

"I can do that," Jane said, trying not to sound eager.

He put a cutting board on the table so she could work sitting, but it felt too awkward to slice that way. She stood on one foot to make nice, even cuts, then prepared the bread for the broiler, aware all the while of the organized way in which he went at things.

"Good morning," Louise said, coming into the kitchen dressed for the day in a tan cotton skirt and a crisply ironed blouse in a pleasing sand shade. She looked so fresh and perky that Jane felt a bit frumpy in jeans and a roomy, gray sweatshirt. "What can I do to help?"

"You can stand the napkins on the plates. I've already folded them into fans. Then it's not too soon to pour the orange juice. Oh, and if you have time, I noticed the tablecloth hangs a few inches longer on one end than the other. Maybe you can straighten it, then rearrange the table settings."

"I'm done. Is there anything else I can do?" Jane asked.

"You just relax, Janey. There's not another thing to do at the moment."

An eighty-year-old friend had once told Jane that the world seemed to be passing her by. Jane was a long way from being elderly, but she felt the same way this morning. It really didn't matter whether she was there or not. She longed to get back to cooking.

She retreated to the library and her spot on the cot. It did feel good to elevate her leg on a pillow and lean back. She needed to come up with something to keep herself occupied.

Her father's library contained many books, but she'd rarely had time to do anything but dust them. From where she was sitting, she could make out some of the titles on the shelves. This was a golden opportunity to do some reading.

Now, where to begin? Something light would be nice, although she wasn't optimistic about finding a novel in her father's collection that would hold her interest. He had especially enjoyed Shakespeare, rereading favorite plays until he could quote a multitude of the speeches. Unfortunately, Jane's classroom introduction to *Julius Caesar* and *Macbeth* hadn't encouraged her to try other plays, and she wasn't in the mood for daggers or witches this morning.

What was she thinking? It wasn't as if she didn't have any responsibilities. It would be embarrassing if Louise asked to see the account book. Jane had taken it out several times— every day, in fact—but somehow there was always an interruption or an excuse not to make the entries. Her sister's system was so orderly and clear that it should have been simple to keep it up-to-date. Jane knew that she was guilty of procrastination.

She hobbled over to the desk, leaving her crutches where they were. Even though it was slow going, she really needed to depend on them less. Every other time she'd intended to work on the books, she'd propped them on a lap pillow. No wonder she couldn't get on with the financial affairs of the inn. Good business procedures demanded that she work on a hard, flat surface.

Before beginning on the accounts, she read over the list of people who'd agreed to pick up trash. That list wasn't very long, considering that they had a whole mile to cover on both sides of the highway. Fortunately, she had more members to call, but she put the church directory aside for now. It was too early in the morning to phone.

Louise used a fountain pen because she enjoyed the clean, crisp lines that were possible with one of the implements from Father's collection. Jane debated whether to use the gold-plated one made by the Sheaffer Pen Company and engraved with his name or the mock tortoise-shell Parker pen. She filled them both with black ink from a bottle kept in the desk and took out a clean sheet of paper to test them.

The Sheaffer produced a bold stroke, perhaps a little too broad for the account ledger. The Parker had a finer point, but she picked up the gold pen again because she loved the feel of it in her hand. Just for fun, she turned the two random strokes into the beginning of a drawing.

Without too much conscious thought, she began drawing a rough sketch of the kitchen with Salty flipping a pancake into the air. She didn't have any trouble capturing the shape of his head with his short crew cut or the crinkle lines by his eyes. His nose was a little tricky. It was wide, but not unpleasantly so, and she didn't want her drawing to be in any way offensive. She was working on the anchor tattoo on his arm when Alice poked her head into the library.

"Good morning, Jane. Louise and I are going to have breakfast now. Won't you join us?"

Jane quickly opened a desk drawer and slid the drawing into it, being careful not to smear any ink that was still damp. There was no serious reason to hide it from Alice, but it seemed like such an idle way to pass time. If it turned out well, she could show it to her later.

Alice was scheduled to begin work at three PM, not the most convenient shift since it meant she would be away at the same time that Louise was occupied with after-school lessons. To make up for her absence, she tried to accomplish as much as possible in the morning.

She'd forgotten to mention the chimney guard to her sisters, and she wanted to do so, but Louise was busy giving Salty his lesson. They hadn't closed the parlor door, so she could hear him pinging on the piano and singing at the top of his lungs. She recognized some World War I songs, but she thought that "He's a Doughboy from Ohio" must be the original composition by his grandfather. Salty certainly belted it out with enthusiasm. Alice resisted the temptation to close the parlor door.

She decided to see how Jane was doing and went to see her in the library. Surprisingly, the room was empty, and the same was true in the living room, dining room and kitchen.

The weather was balmy, perfect for late May, but Jane wasn't on the front porch. Alice remembered her own offer to do some outdoor jobs and went to the spacious garden, wondering if perhaps Jane was there planning what she wanted done to get it ready for summer. Her sister wasn't there either. All Alice saw there was work waiting for her attention. Maybe after lunch she would have time to spade a bed for spring plantings. She needed to get Jane's input on what should go there, then buy some flats at the nursery another day.

Where was Jane? It was a big house, but one didn't get lost in it as a rule, especially not a sister on crutches who wouldn't dream of taking a nap before noon.

Jane was having fun. It felt so good to sketch that she wanted to try her hand at something a little nicer. She kept a pad of acid-free paper on her closet shelf along with miscellaneous art supplies that had lain neglected for some time. She liked what she'd done with the drawing of Salty and decided to do a more refined version.

It was a bit risky carrying the ink bottle and pens in the pockets of her jeans, but she got up to her bedroom without mishap. After setting up on a small writing desk, she lightly sketched a scene similar to the first one using pencil, erasing and redoing it until it looked right to her. Then she went over the lines in ink. The pancake flipping hadn't looked quite right, so she had Salty carrying a huge platter stacked chin-high with his creations.

Naturally, it would have been easier to draw him if he were there to pose, but she wanted this to be a surprise, a going-away memento for all the work he was doing. Maybe she would add a bit of color, either with her watercolors or pencils.

It was some time later that she remembered the trash pickup. She had to have a crew ready in two days to fill Jack's borrowed truck with debris. She had calls to make and bookkeeping to do, but it wouldn't hurt to work just a little longer on her picture.

Alice couldn't remember the last time she'd been so busy at the hospital. Or maybe it just seemed that way because she was concerned about what was happening at the inn. She'd tried to call Jane on her break, but the phone was busy.

After driving home from the hospital, she parked her car on the street and went up the front walk, too weary to enjoy the star-studded sky above her or the scent of lilacs in the air. On nights that she worked late, she used the front door rather than make her way around the house in the dark. Usually, though, Jane turned on the porch light for her. Tonight there was no welcoming glow. She carefully went up the steps, the blackness broken only by the light spilling out from the foyer.

"Don't be frightened," a soft voice said. "We're here on the porch."

Alice was startled, but she squinted to see who had spoken.

"It's such a nice night. Henry and I are sitting here enjoying it."

"Emily," she said, recognizing their guest. "Don't let me disturb you. I'm just coming home from work."

"I'm glad you're here. I'd like you to meet my friend."

"Let me turn on the light," Alice said, finding the outside switch.

The glow from the bulb above brought out the Victorian ambiance of the porch, and now she could see the tall, slender man standing beside Emily. He had dark hair graying at the temples and wore glasses with narrow wire frames. He was a handsome man in the old-fashioned sense of the word with a patrician nose, well-formed mouth and kind-looking eyes.

"Miss Howard," Henry Toyer said when they were introduced. "It's a pleasure. Emily spoke very highly of your hospitality. I've heard Grace Chapel Inn mentioned often in Potterston, and apparently your reputation isn't exaggerated."

"Thank you, and please do call me Alice. I'm glad you're enjoying the porch. I love sitting out here on warm evenings. It's so peaceful."

"That it is," Henry agreed. "If I weren't so attached to Potterston, Acorn Hill is the place I would want to live."

Emily was quiet, and Alice knew enough about her situation to know that she wasn't longing for the tranquility of a town this small.

"I thought I'd have a cup of herbal tea before bed," Alice said. "Could I bring some out for you?"

"Thank you, but I have to be getting home. I have to change all the locks in an apartment building beginning early tomorrow morning," Henry said. "The owner's master key is missing, and he's concerned about security."

"Oh dear, that doesn't sound good," Alice said. She wished him well and they exchanged good-byes.

Alice went ahead to the kitchen and put the kettle on, leaving Emily to say good-night to her friend.

Before the water boiled, Emily came into the kitchen. "I've decided to accept your invitation for tea."

She looked particularly pretty in a silky dress with small turquoise, white and blue flowers on a navy background. Her hair was pulled back and held with a silver comb. A charm bracelet emphasized the slenderness of her wrist. Her face, though, was pale and troubled.

"If there's one thing my sister has, it's a good collection of tea," Alice said, putting two mugs on the table. "I can offer chamomile, hibiscus—that's best with a slice of lemon—red clover, spearmint or citrus blend. That one has a nice cinnamon taste."

"So many choices," Emily said with a light laugh. "I'm

afraid I'm not good at making up my mind. Just surprise me."

"I think I'll go with this one," Alice said, indicating a bright-red box. "It's supposed to provide good dreams while you sleep."

"I'll be happy if I sleep at all." Emily gave her a wan smile. "I came here to make a decision, and I couldn't be further from it if I were on the other side of the world. In fact, I'm more conflicted than ever."

Alice waited, not wanting to press her guest.

"Mr. Toyer seems like a very nice person," she said when the silence between them started to seem uncomfortable.

"He's a wonderful man—considerate, thoughtful, generous, kind, patient. There aren't enough adjectives to do him justice. Oh, I don't know what to do. I'm being so unfair to him."

"Unfair?"

"I should give him an answer, one way or the other, yes or no. He doesn't deserve to be kept in suspense. He wants me to marry him, Alice. He doesn't care whether it's next week or next year. He just wants us to be together, and part of me wants that very much. I don't know what to do."

The tea that Alice had poured was cooling in front of her, but she didn't seem to notice.

"It must be a terribly hard decision," Alice said, not feeling at all qualified to give advice. But then, maybe the best thing she could do was listen without offering an opinion.

"It's impossible. People come to our dental clinics, their teeth in dreadful condition and their gums severely infected. Often it's the only time in their lives that they've had any care. They come in pain, their total well-being impaired by poor dental health." She smiled weakly. "I know, if I leave my job, someone else will take my place. But I've spent years working with aid groups to set up the facilities we need and with private donors to keep the project going. I don't know if I could ever have peace of mind, knowing that even one child is denied care because I wasn't doing my job."

"I understand," Alice said thoughtfully. "I know the hospital will continue to give excellent care long after I retire, but I still feel that I make a difference sometimes."

"I imagine you're an exceptionally caring nurse. You're certainly kind to sit here listening to me at this time of night. You're probably exhausted from all your responsibilities. I don't know how you manage an inn and work at your profession."

"Running the inn is very much a group effort, but I'm afraid my sister Jane does more than her share. Since she's been sidelined with her injured leg, Louise and I are learning just how much she does do."

"It's not a bad thing, knowing where you belong and what you should be doing. I felt that way until I fell in love with Henry. There, I've said it, haven't I? I do love him. I hate to think of not having him in my life, but he deserves more than I'm able to give him right now. He's never married. He has a big family, brothers, sisters, nephews, nieces, an elderly mother in assisted living, aunts and uncles. Henry has always been the dependable one in the family, the person who not only kept the locksmith shop going but expanded it. Half of his relatives work in businesses that he either started or financed. Sometimes I see a loneliness in him that makes me want to cry."

"Things can be very complicated, can't they?" Alice said sympathetically.

"That's not the half of it. Even if Henry were willing to sell his business and live with me in Chicago, we would still be apart much of the time. He'd be there alone while I traveled for my job."

"Is there any chance he would travel with you?"

"Almost none," Emily said with a rueful smile. "He's terrified of flying. He won't even fly to Chicago to see me. He makes that long drive whenever he can, but he won't step on a plane. He even saw a therapist, hoping to get over it, but it's a deep-seated phobia. I wouldn't want him to torture himself on my account. Even if he did make himself fly on big commercial planes, I travel on whatever is available, even a two-seater. I've flown on relics that look like they're held together with chewing gum."

"That does sound dangerous." Alice had a hard time picturing this delicate woman as an adventurer.

"I worry more about the people we're helping than my safety. I'm afraid that concerns Henry a great deal, but it seems so unfair that some have so little and we have so much." She took a sip of tea that had to be too cool by now. "Here I am, keeping you up after your long day."

"I always need some time to unwind before bed," Alice assured her. "Would you like me to warm your tea? I'm going to have a second cup myself."

"Thank you. It's sweet of you to listen to my troubles. Henry is a nice man, don't you think?"

"Yes, he seems the kind of person you trust instinctively. Perhaps there's a way to work things out." She spoke optimistically for Emily's sake, but she was afraid that sometimes a relationship just wasn't meant to be.

"I have made one decision," Emily said with a faint smile. "If Henry and I aren't meant to be together, I have to let him go. It's not fair to him to leave things as they are now."

Chapter Eight

J ane had disappeared again. Alice didn't need her for any particular reason, but she thought it odd that she wasn't in the library resting.

The phone rang for the fifth time in a half hour, and Alice picked it up at the registration desk. This time it was her aunt.

"Aunt Ethel, it's nice to hear from you. Are you enjoying yourself?"

Ordinarily, her aunt would answer a question like that in great detail, but this morning she was focused on something else.

"I told Jane to call me every day and let me know how she's doing. Here it is Wednesday, and I haven't heard a word since Monday. I would be happy to call her, but it doesn't seem fair to run up a big long-distance charge on my son's phone."

She sounded hurt and perhaps a bit perturbed. If there was one thing that upset Ethel, it was being out of the loop. She loved knowing everyone's business, although she was never malicious in her quest to know and spread gossip.

"Jane's been on the phone a lot getting volunteers for the chapel's highway-cleaning project."

"Why would anyone clean a highway?"

"They're not cleaning the pavement, only the sides of the road. Different community groups have agreed to help. Jane is cochair of the chapel's committee. Since she won't be able to participate herself, she's working hard to get enough people."

"Why would anyone volunteer to do such dirty work? There's no telling what people throw along the road. Don't they have prisoners to do work like that?"

"I don't know about prisoners, but there are so many miles of highway in Pennsylvania that every community could offer help. We are stewards of God's earth."

"Yes, I guess so. Can I talk to Jane now?"

"You could, but I'm not sure where she is."

"How could you lose her? Surely she can't go far on crutches."

"I'll have her call you, Aunt Ethel. Maybe she's taking a shower or a nap."

"A nap? That doesn't sound like Jane, not in the middle of the morning."

Alice had to agree.

"Oh, Alice, have you been checking my house every day? I imagine everything is fine, but I do feel better if someone looks in."

Their aunt had lived in the carriage house by the inn since selling the farmhouse she'd shared with her late husband. It was a good arrangement, allowing the sisters to keep tabs on her. She enjoyed the social life in Acorn Hill a great deal after the solitude that went with being a farmer's wife. Much as Ethel loved visiting her three children, she did seem to get homesick for the little town where she'd lived for ten years.

Truth to tell, Alice had forgotten about checking the carriage house. Now that she'd been reminded, it still didn't seem terribly important. In cold weather, they would have monitored the heat, but on these lovely spring days, there was no urgency.

"We've been lax, I'm afraid. Louise and I are both struggling to get everything done. We didn't realize how much Jane does to keep the inn going. But I'll go check for you right away."

"Thank you, Alice. And please do tell Jane to call me as soon as she can. I can't imagine what your sister does to keep busy while she's laid up. I rarely see her sitting, let alone lying around all day."

"She's been keeping herself occupied," Alice assured her. "She repaired an old tablecloth, and she's keeping the inn's books up to date to help Louise."

"That doesn't sound like enough to fill her days."

Again, Alice had to agree with Ethel. She'd been so busy doing some of Jane's jobs that she hadn't considered how bored Jane must be. But for the moment, she couldn't even find Jane, let alone sympathize with her. She hurried off to check their aunt's little home, thinking of all the other things to get done that day.

When she got back, she heard Salty belting out the words of his grandfather's song once again. She peeked into the parlor, taking care not to disturb the lesson in progress.

"I think it might be easier if you didn't sing while you play," Louise was saying in a tactful voice. "Once you have it right, you can sing along."

Alice didn't want to insult Salty by shutting the parlor door, but she certainly sympathized with her sister. It couldn't be easy to give a lesson to an adult who was more focused on performing than on learning.

She stood in the foyer for a few moments, trying to make a mental list of all the jobs that needed doing. Every time she thought of one task, two related ones came to mind. She felt a bit guilty for wishing the hospital would call her to work. There, at least, she knew exactly what was expected of her.

Looking up as someone came down the stairs, Alice was glad to see it was Emily. After their conversation last night, Alice had thought a lot about her guest's dilemma.

"Good morning, Emily. Did you miss breakfast this morning?"

"Yes, but it doesn't matter. I tossed and turned last night before I finally got to sleep. Not because the bed isn't comfortable or the room restful, I just had—you understand—things on my mind. But I have to tell you something. There's water on the floor in the hallway."

"Water? On the floor?" Alice felt a bit dull repeating what Emily had just said, but she couldn't imagine how it could be true on the second floor. It was a nice sunny day, but even if it were raining, an open window or leaking roof wasn't likely to cause water in the hallway.

"I thought you would want to know." Emily obviously was uncomfortable about bringing bad news.

"Yes, I'll take a look."

She hurried up the stairs and quickly saw what Emily meant. A trickle of water was coming from under the door of the Garden Room.

"Not Bert Frame again!" she said aloud, rushing downstairs for the master key.

Emily followed her back up and sounded as distressed as Alice felt when they saw the dampened carpet inside the bedroom.

Hurrying into the bathroom, Alice's worst fear was confirmed. The tap in the sink hadn't been turned off all the way. A thin trickle of water was dribbling into the bowl and overflowing onto the floor. Not only had their careless guest left the water partially on, he had managed to plug up the sink. The stopper was up, so there was no reason why the water shouldn't have drained. Somehow he had blocked the pipe.

Alice gave the faucet handle a hard turn and stopped the flow of water, then turned her attention to the potential damage. Her first thought was to save the hardwood floor in the hallway. She grabbed the room's stack of clean towels and raced out to soak up the water. Thanks to Emily, she'd caught it before there was noticeable damage, but cleaning up the bedroom and bath wouldn't be so easy.

"What can I do?" Emily asked. "Maybe if we roll up the carpet."

"I can't ask you to help. You're a guest," Alice said as she frantically tried to move the heavy, water-soaked floor covering.

"You can't do that alone." Emily bent beside her and together they managed to begin rolling it.

"I think the carpet has absorbed most of the water," Emily said, kneeling even though the water was soaking her slim-line blue linen skirt.

"It's too heavy for us," Alice said. "I'll have to get someone to move the furniture to get the carpeting up. I hope it hasn't leaked through to the ceiling.

"Oh dear, Emily, you've ruined your skirt," she said, feeling overwhelmed by the mess their careless guest had made.

"Don't give it a thought. It's fully washable."

"I have to check downstairs and get help."

Alice rushed down the steps, almost slipping because the soles of her shoes were wet. She clutched the banister, knowing what a disaster it would be if she were injured too.

"Louise, we have a flood in Bert Frame's room," she said, interrupting the lesson in the parlor. "He left the faucet dribbling into the sink and somehow managed to stop up the drain. Do you see any water leaking through to the ceiling down here?"

Salty broke off abruptly in the middle of playing the doughboy song and looked upward.

"Looks dry to me. Let's see what he did."

Before Alice could say another word, both he and Louise were hurrying up the stairs.

"Be careful, it's slippery in there," Emily warned. She'd started to clear out the room by carrying out the small bedside table.

"What are we going to do with that man?" Louise cried out in distress.

"He'd better shape up or ship out," Salty said, sizing up the problem and starting to move the dresser aside. "We need all the rags and mops you can find. I'll start to pull up this rug and see how much damage has been done."

Louise hurried down to the storage room for supplies, followed by Emily, while Alice gathered all the dusting rags and worn towels kept at the bottom of the linen closet. She got down on her hands and knees to dry the hallway, afraid one of the helpers would slip on the still-damp surface.

Before Louise could return, Salty directed Alice to help him dismantle the bed. She took an end of the mattress to carry it out, but he seemed to be taking most of the weight on himself. It took her a minute to notice that Jane had shown up and was standing with her crutches, watching all the damage control.

"How can I help?" she asked, although no one had an answer for her.

While Louise tackled the wet floor in the bathroom, squeezing out the mop in a bucket, Emily carried small items, including Bert Frame's luggage, from the room. Alice helped Salty with furniture. Fortunately she was used to lifting at the hospital and was able to move the heavier pieces.

She was terribly upset that a guest had been so careless. How could he leave a tap on and not notice? What did he do to stop up the drain? The man had a lot to answer for, and it was going to be a test of her faith to forgive him.

At Salty's suggestion, they threw the roll of wet carpeting through the window rather than try to drag it down the stairs and through the foyer, leaving a wet trail behind. Alice was pretty sure it was a complete loss. Even if they rolled it out to dry in the sun, it would never be the same. It was stained and might foster mold.

"I don't know how I'll ever thank you," Alice said to Emily and Salty as they continued to work on the cleanup. "We've never had anything like this happen at the inn."

The bedroom was stripped bare, and the bathroom had been scrubbed down, but both rooms needed to air out and dry before more could be done. Water was sitting in the sink, and Salty's attempt to clear the drain by poking it with a straightened wire hanger was totally unsuccessful.

"I'll have to call a plumber," Alice said, her mind a blank regarding the name of the man they usually used.

"I can do that," Jane offered, still hovering in the hallway on her crutches. "I'll go downstairs and do it now."

Alice's first instinct was to spare her sister, but she'd seen how Jane watched over them as they worked. She and Louise might be overworked at the moment, but Jane was suffering more, not being able to help.

"Yes, please do. But be careful on the steps. I can't guarantee that we didn't track any water on them."

She looked at her wristwatch, noticing that they were well into the afternoon. She wondered when new guests would arrive. Could they possibly have everything put right before the first one checked in?

"I'd like to help more," Salty said, "but I promised to take Hope to a dentist appointment when she gets off work. Her car is in the shop."

"I don't know what we would have done without you," Alice said, giving him her heartfelt thanks.

He looked a bit embarrassed by the gratitude she and Louise heaped on him, showing Alice a new side of the brusque, no-nonsense chef. Louise accompanied him to the door, expressing more appreciation as they walked.

"Oh, Emily," Alice said with distress, "Have we ruined your plans for the day?"

"Not at all. Henry has a busy day today, changing locks on all those apartments. I didn't plan to see him until we have dinner this evening. Sorry as I am for the damage to your room, it was a positive distraction for me."

"I hope things go well for you," Alice said, feeling sympathy for her new friend at the same time that she felt drained by the crisis.

Emily went to her room to shower and change clothes, and Alice joined her sisters in the kitchen for a few badly needed moments of relaxation. Louise had the kettle going when she got there, and Jane was sitting at the table, lost in her own thoughts.

"Did you have any luck with the plumber?" Alice asked.

"Oh yes." Jane blinked as though surfacing from a world of her own. "I called Mr. Villeneuve and told him what a mess we have. He's agreed to come as soon as he finishes another job. He couldn't be specific about the time."

"Mr. Villeneuve, that's an elegant name for a plumber," Louise mused.

"I call him Mr. V," Jane admitted. "I can't seem to get my tongue around all those vowels, and I don't want to insult him by mispronouncing it."

"I'm feeling a bit ashamed of myself," Louise said, pouring hot water over the spearmint tea bags in a china pot with tiny hand-painted violets.

"Whatever for?" Jane asked.

"I rather dread Salty's lessons. He's not very interested in learning to play better. What he really wants is an audience for the songs he loves, especially his grandfather's. I find myself wishing for ear plugs after the fourth or fifth time through 'He's a Doughboy from Ohio.'"

"I only hear it in passing, and it does get a little monotonous," Alice said. "But you're living up to your agreement. He seems satisfied."

"Yes, I suppose, but I'm only making a halfhearted effort

to teach him. And look how helpful he is. Moving all that furniture and helping with the cleanup. Whenever we've needed him, he's right there helping. I shouldn't begrudge him a little of my time. If only he would try to improve the way he plays that doughboy song instead of belting it out at the top of his lungs."

"I'm not sure I know exactly what a doughboy is," Jane said. "I assume it has something to do with baking."

"Salty has been giving me lessons about that," Louise said with a laugh. "The word originated way back when Napoleon was making war. British sailors and soldiers called the fried dumplings that their cooks prepared doughboys. The U. S. army picked it up during the Mexican-American War and used it to refer to the shape of the infantry's uniform buttons. It's hard to trace the exact origin of words."

"Not that much to do with food? I'm disappointed," Jane said.

"Well, maybe. Others say it had to do with the way they cooked flour and rice rations, either in the ashes of campfires or on the ends of bayonets. Anyway, they used the word doughboy in the Civil War too."

"I thought it was what they called soldiers in World War I," Alice said, intrigued even though she'd never had much interest in military things.

"According to Salty—and he seems really up on the subject—doughboy came to mean all the troops sent to Europe in World War I. It was a proud name then. It lost all its negative connotations."

"Well, it seems you're the one getting lessons," Alice teased. "Is Salty learning anything? I mostly hear him singing."

Louise grimaced. "He remembers more from his music lessons as a child than I expected, but we haven't made any progress to speak of. He's not patient with scales and doesn't like practicing basic pieces. He's totally focused on his World

War I songs. I'm not criticizing: It's a unique way of honoring his grandfather's memory and the sacrifices his family has made. It's just that I'm not really helping him."

"Well, he certainly seems to be enjoying himself," Jane said.

"Yes, that's something, isn't it?"

"And we certainly need him," Alice said. "I never expected to say it about anyone besides Father, but it's nice to have a man around this house."

"Especially when we have bats and floods," Louise said.

After their short break, Louise went to get ready for her students, and Jane prepared to call more chapel members.

They'd agreed not to have dinner until after the plumber came. Alice insisted on showing him the stopped-up sink herself, not wanting Jane to make an unnecessary trip up the stairs. Her sister was getting proficient on crutches, but it still made her nervous to see Jane's slow ascent. She knew of a number of patients at the hospital who'd fallen using crutches, and she didn't want Jane to be a casualty.

Although she told herself it was silly, Alice was never totally comfortable dealing with workmen who came to the house. She knew that it was wise to get estimates ahead of time, but she was never sure whether to insist.

Home repairs were a minor concern compared to the problem of Bert Frame. Should he be asked to leave? Jane thought so. Or should she insist that he pay for the ruined carpet? Louise suggested adding the cost to his bill. He seemed like such an inoffensive little man, but he was a walking disaster when it came to common sense things like windows and faucets. Was he really that absentminded, or was he troubled by something that distracted him from everyday responsibilities? Either way, she had to talk to him as soon as he returned to the inn.

She had no idea what to say, and the more she thought about it, the bigger the problem seemed. She didn't want to be unfair, but they simply couldn't have a guest who left chaos in his wake.

It was after six o'clock when Mr. Villeneuve arrived. Alice wondered whether he charged double for evening work, but she didn't ask when she realized that they needed him even if he did. She could pronounce his name in her head, but Jane had spooked her a bit. She avoided calling him anything because "Mr. V" seemed too familiar for a man she'd never met. It hit home again how many details of running the inn fell to Jane.

"It's up here, sir," she said, leading the way. "I'm afraid one of our guests has been terribly careless. Not only did he stop up the sink, he left the water flowing into it. We had quite a mess before it was noticed."

The plumber grunted as if to say that he'd heard it all before.

In the bathroom he put down his huge box full of tools and started spreading them around. Alice didn't know whether to watch or leave. Would he resent having her look over his shoulder? She felt rather inadequate, trying to remember how her father had handled workmen. In fact, he had always been interested in what they were doing, which was probably why he always supervised home repairs himself.

Mr. Villeneuve was a large man with massive shoulders and legs like tree trunks. He seemed to fill the small bathroom as he tackled the drain with a tool that Alice had never seen before. She felt crowded out and quietly made her way back downstairs.

Louise was in the kitchen fixing canned soup and grilled cheese sandwiches for dinner. Jane was making a few calls to people who could only be reached during the supper hour. Alice hovered in the hallway, feeling that she should be with the plumber but reluctant to get in his way.

"Good evening, Miss Howard."

She spun around to find their notorious guest, Bert Frame.

"Mr. Frame, I was just thinking about you." This wasn't strictly true at the moment, but he certainly had been on her mind most of the day.

"I'm sure I closed the windows when I left this morning." He looked frazzled with his mud-colored tie hanging loose over a wrinkled yellow dress shirt. His suit jacket was bunched in one hand and his briefcase hung from the other. Alice would have pitied his look of exhaustion if she hadn't been so annoyed by his carelessness.

"That's not the problem today. Your sink was stopped up."

"Yes, I did notice that it wasn't draining well. I meant to tell you, but I was late and forgot. I'm terribly sorry."

"Mr. Frame, you didn't turn off the water all the way. It overflowed the sink and soaked through the bedroom carpet. Another guest noticed water in the hall."

"Oh dear." He looked so distressed that she didn't know what to say next.

The plumber came downstairs before she could speak.

"Here's the trouble, Missus." He was holding up a little pink plastic pick, the kind used to hold a wire hair roller in place. "It got caught in the pipe and gunk built up around it. Could have been in there quite a long time. The drain's fine now."

He held out the offending pick, but she kept her hands at her sides, not wanting to handle something that had been trapped in a drain.

"Shall I write you a check?" she asked.

"I'll send a bill. I've done work here before. Rev. Howard always had me ream out the pipe to the sewer every five years or so. Heads off trouble. Tree roots work their way in. Wouldn't be a bad idea if I take care of that sometime soon. Nasty business when your main outlet backs up."

Alice could imagine the problems they would have if the plumbing malfunctioned with a house full of guests.

"Maybe you'd better do that."

"Since it's not an emergency, I may not get to it for a couple of weeks. I'll call you before I come."

"Yes, please do."

Mr. Villeneuve left through the front door, but Bert Frame was still hovering nearby. Alice was in a total quandary now. She had agreed with her sisters that he should leave after tonight, but obviously the hair pick that had caused the drain stoppage had nothing to do with him. Still, he had been careless not reporting it. Was it his responsibility, or could a guest reasonably assume that someone would notice the clog when the room was cleaned?

No matter what the cause of the stopped sink, he had left the water running. Even a dribble was enough to cause serious damage when it didn't drain away.

"It's all my fault. I should have made sure the water was off all the way," he said penitently. "I'll be happy to pay for the plumber and replace your carpet. I'm afraid I do tend to be absentminded when I have a big deal in the works. There are always snags and holdups, and my company expects me to cut through them like a hot knife through butter."

Alice knew the sensible thing was to have a conference with her sisters to decide how to handle the situation. She also knew that Jane made decisions like this all the time, taking responsibility because she and Louise were too busy.

They'd never asked a guest to leave, but then, they'd never had one like Bert Frame. Would he cause more problems if he stayed out his reservation? Could she put all the blame on him when it was the innkeepers' responsibility to have everything in working order?

She looked into his face and saw the dark circles under his eyes and the way his mouth sagged at the corners. His shoulders drooped with fatigue, and she had a strong feeling that he carried more responsibility than he could comfortably handle. She knew nothing of his personal life, but his shirt looked as if it had never been ironed. It wasn't just creased from a day's wear. His suit pants were badly in need of a good pressing too, and his shoes hadn't seen any polish in some time. Worse, his skin seemed sallow, to her nurse's mind a sign that his health wasn't what it should be.

It wasn't her place to suggest that he go in for a physical with his doctor, but, given his haggard appearance, she simply didn't have the heart to throw him out. Surely he would be extra careful after the incident with the faucet. Anyway, he would be leaving on his own soon. She made the decision to let him stay and hoped her sisters wouldn't be upset.

"The plumbing is our responsibility," she said. "There's no reason for you to pay for repairs at the inn."

"The carpet—" he began.

"Maybe we'll just put down some throw rugs," she said, although the idea had just occurred to her. "It is a pretty hardwood floor."

"Yes, Grace Chapel Inn is beautiful," he said, "but it's my fault the sink overflowed."

"Let's just forget it for now."

She was relieved when he went up to his room, but she still had to tell her sisters what she'd done.

They were waiting for her arrival before they began supper, but she wouldn't have an appetite until she admitted what she'd decided.

"The stopped sink wasn't Mr. Frame's fault. The plumber found a pick from a woman's hair curler in the drain. I couldn't in good conscience hold him responsible."

"He did leave the water running," Jane said.

"It's his fault the carpet was ruined." Louise was slicing their sandwiches and putting them on a serving platter. Alice noticed that they were a bit charred around the edges.

"Actually, he offered to pay the plumber's bill and buy a new carpet."

"We couldn't let him pay the plumber, but it seems only fair that he replace the carpet," Louise said.

"Did you ask him to leave tomorrow?" Jane asked.

"Well, not exactly."

"You're letting him stay," Louise said in a matter-of-fact way.

"You're not going to let him replace the carpet," Jane said, registering no surprise.

Alice shook her head as her sisters burst into laughter.

"Our dear Alice," Louise said.

"They weren't good decisions?" Alice asked unhappily.

"Hey, they were yours to make. You never second-guess me," Jane said, "and I certainly won't fault you."

"There are a couple of little things I should tell you."

"Oh?" Louise started spooning out a rather watery chicken noodle soup.

"When the bat man was here, he told me it would be a good idea to have a guard put on our chimney. It will keep out critters. Some, like raccoons, can be a real problem. I told him to go ahead."

"How much will it cost?" Louise asked.

"I'm afraid I forgot to ask. And one other thing. The plumber said that Father had the sewer line reamed out every so many years, and we're overdue. I told him to do it."

"And you didn't ask what that will cost," Jane said in a neutral voice.

"I didn't think of it until after he left."

Louise raised her eyebrows and Jane shook her head and sighed. Then they both smiled.

Alice had never felt more grateful for their loving partnership, but she fervently hoped that things would get back to normal soon.

Chapter Nine

L ouise looked at her wardrobe with misgivings Thursday morning. What did one wear to pick up trash? She didn't own a pair of jeans, and unfortunately any she might borrow from either of her sisters would not fit right.

She explored the back of the closet, wondering why on earth she had saved so many outdated garments. Her suits, skirts and blouses were mostly classic in design, aging gracefully, but that certainly wasn't true of the white eyelet peasant blouse or a striped lavender and green tunic. She felt a twinge of nostalgia when she took out a long black evening gown that she'd worn to concerts with her late husband in Philadelphia. Even if she never wore the gown again, she wasn't ready to part with it.

There had to be something old but still serviceable. She pulled out a turquoise crocheted skirt, handmade by a friend many years ago. She'd worn it only once because it clung in a most unflattering way. It was past time to donate it to a charity. She started a pile of discards on her bed and added the navy ruffled skirt that went with the peasant blouse.

Tempting as it was to go through her whole wardrobe and sort out things to give away, she still had to find something to wear. She found nothing, and with her sisters' permission, moved on to their closets. Alice's jeans fit her in the waist but were too short. Louise wanted to make sure that she was protected as much as possible from the tall roadside grass and what might be lurking in it, so she explored Jane's offerings. Her youngest sister's jeans were long enough, but proved to be too snug. She finally settled on Jane's gardening overalls with a long-sleeved T-shirt and a straw hat to shade her from the sun. After she was dressed, she looked in the mirror and laughed. It seemed not only was she filling Jane's shoes on the clean-up detail, she was dressed entirely like her. She descended the stairs with a smile on her face and headed to the kitchen for a quick breakfast.

Salty took it personally when any one of them bypassed his breakfast. Fortunately all the guests were fed by the time she came downstairs, and he had enough blueberry pancakes left over to give her a quick meal.

"They'll be better if I cook some up fresh," he said.

"No, these are lovely. I have to be at the chapel at eight o'clock. Remember, I won't be back in time for your lesson. You're welcome to come for one in the evening if you like."

"I'll just practice on my own today, if that's okay. You'll be tired after a day of cleaning up."

"No doubt, but I'll be back for my lessons before the first student comes at four."

She had a hard time imagining a whole day spent along the side of the road, but Jack said he only expected them to work until the truck was full. Then he would leave for the dump and borrow it another day if necessary.

The plan was to meet at the chapel and go out to the highway in as many cars as they needed. Jane had assured her that she didn't need to be one of the drivers, so she walked over, grateful that the sun was shining and the temperature was moderate. It was good that they were doing this before the weather became uncomfortably warm.

Jane, after having made a major, last-minute effort at recruiting, had seemed satisfied with the number of volunteers, and Louise was pleased to see a sizeable group gathered in the parking lot. What she hadn't expected was that, at age sixty-five, she was one of the younger ones. Of course, on a weekday most people had to be at their jobs, but she was still surprised by the number of senior citizens who had turned out.

One whose presence was particularly unexpected was Harvey Racklin, a longtime member of the chapel. She couldn't remember the crusty octogenarian ever volunteering for a project. He was the congregation's naysayer, always vocal when it came to any kind of change, but never raising his hand to help. Perhaps he thought it was especially important to take care of the environment.

Even more surprising, Byrdie Hutchinson was there. Many people thought she was rather dour, but Louise knew she had a good heart. Her natural reserve made her seem unsociable at times, and it was totally unlike her to join with the others in a group project. Jane must have been very persuasive to get her to help.

There were a few people that Louise knew only by name, but for the most part, the volunteers were longtime members. Louise was gratified to see Justine Gilmore, a single mother who struggled to earn enough to raise her eight-year-old daughter. She knew that of all the people there, she was making the greatest sacrifice to help. Louise was reminded of a favorite Bible story, the widow who gave two very small coins to the temple. She remembered what Jesus had said:

"All these people gave their gifts out of their wealth; but she out of her poverty put in all she had to live on" (Luke 21:4).

Her father had always valued gifts of time and talent as highly as treasure. Louise realized that they all had a calling to care for God's creation. She was glad to be there. Her duties at the inn would wait.

Jack O'Hara had a gift for leadership, either by nature or from his time in the marines. He took charge, taking a head count of those who'd showed up to work. Jack was the only man she knew who could look spruce in faded jeans, a plaid work shirt and a baseball cap.

"We're all here, folks. Rachel and Harvey have volunteered to transport people, and Ronald has room for six more in his van."

He gestured at Florence Simpson's husband, a quiet, patient man who never seemed disturbed by his wife's bombastic personality. Ronald was always present when work was needed on the chapel's building or grounds, and Louise knew he would be an asset today.

"Rev. Thompson said to give you his regrets that he can't be here to help," Jack said before people scattered to the vehicles. "He's scheduled to participate in a retreat and couldn't in good conscience not attend it. But we have a fine group here. Before you get in the cars, take one of the work bundles. There are black bags for trash, white for cans and orange for bottles that can be recycled. Jane Howard is mighty sorry she can't be with us. She's laid up with a leg injury, but she paired everyone up. Each team of two will need a supply of bags, heavy-duty rubber gloves and one of these sticks to pick up trash."

He demonstrated with military thoroughness—although it seemed self-evident—how to pick things up with the metal point on the end.

"If the partners take turns holding bags and picking things up, you can go faster and you shouldn't get as tired. Here are the pairings."

It soon became obvious that Jane had put the oldest and youngest together. She was glad that Justine would be working with Byrdie instead of crabby Harvey Racklin. Rachel Holzmann, co-owner with her husband of Acorn Hill Antiques, would have Harvey as a partner, but she wasn't one to tolerate nastiness.

Louise didn't know her partner very well. Dorothy

Gunnerson was a newcomer to Acorn Hill, having come there with her recently retired husband. They'd spent most of their working years in Pittsburgh and were still adjusting to the small-town pace. This would be a good opportunity to get to know her. Louise's schedule was so full that, regretfully, she didn't always have a chance to welcome new members as she would have liked.

It was decided that they would finish one side of their mile before crossing the highway to begin on the other side, probably a project for another day. With that determined, the group departed, and after a short drive arrived at their destination. The drivers distributed the partners at intervals along the mile stretch. As bags were filled, Jack would pick up the trash, and Ronald would put the recyclables in the back of his van.

"Would you like the first turn holding the bags?" Louise asked.

"Whatever you like," Dorothy Gunnerson said. "Maybe we can change jobs every fifteen minutes. I don't want to come down with arthritis. I'm glad to help, but at my age, one has to be a bit cautious."

Louise didn't think arthritis was something you acquired by working, but she thought it was a good idea to switch off fairly often. Her partner was a bit on the plump side and perhaps unused to exercise. She had a round, friendly face with a fringe of blond bangs just beginning to show some gray. Unlike Louise's ragbag outfit, Dorothy was color coordinated in a pair of tan cotton slacks with a matching jacket over a cocoa-brown knit top.

"I brought my own hand protection," she said, taking a pair of pink flowered gardening mitts from her pocket. "Rubber is so hot. I didn't want sweaty hands. When I garden, I sometimes change gloves three or four times. Nothing shows a woman's age like rough, red hands. When I lived in Pittsburgh, I had a standing appointment to have my nails done. Of course, in a big city, there are so many services

available that you can't get in small towns. I'm not sure how
this retirement is going to work out. We travel to all the places
we didn't have time to see while my husband was working, so
I'll be gone a good share of the time. But he does want a qui-
eter life. I guess he deserves it. He had a very high-power job.
Poor man, it wore him out. He wanted to work another two
years, but I insisted that he get out of the rat race before his
health went. I mean, what's the point of working so hard all
your life if you can't enjoy some leisure?"

Louise tried to prompt her partner to hold the trash bag
open, but she couldn't get a word in edgewise. Her stick was
full of discarded fast-food containers, a big chunk of yellowed
newsprint and something too faded and mushy to identify.

"Uh, Dorothy—"

"Of course, we won't see our children as often as we did
in Pittsburgh. We have three, two of them married. I would
love to have a grandchild, but today's young people are so
pokey about starting a family. I even have names picked out.
If the first one is a boy, I want him named after my brother.
His name is James Madison Masters. I have no idea why my
parents named him after a president—James Madison, I
mean—but James is such a nice name. Of course, I realize that
naming a child is up to the parents, but a grandmother can
make suggestions, can't she? My brother is such a love. He
didn't have children, so there's no one to be his namesake.
Not that his wife isn't a lovely woman. Andrea and I—"

"Dorothy, I really need you to hold the garbage sack open.
I see some aluminum cans over there. They go in the white bag."

"Are you sure? I thought cans go in orange."

"No, glass goes in the orange."

The pair of workers ahead of them had already done several yards and widened the gap between them.

"Well, my husband says I'm a better talker than a lis-
tener. I always do like a good conversation. When I was in
kindergarten . . ."

Louise emptied her first load into the bag, trying not to be overwhelmed by Dorothy's nonstop flow of words. She picked up a pair of cans, gingerly dumping out some liquid that she hoped was only rainwater, then her eye caught sight of a shining bit of metal. She walked over expecting it to be foil or a tab from one of the cans.

"Well, look at this," she said, inadvertently interrupting Dorothy's latest monologue. "Someone has lost a locket."

She rubbed clinging dirt from the surface with the finger of her glove and held it up. It was a pretty gold-colored heart with a design engraved on it. It looked like the kind of sentimental trinket that someone would regret losing.

"Now how on earth did that get out here?" Dorothy said, peering at it with interest. "I wonder if it's collectible. I guess that would depend on how old it is. Are we allowed to keep things we find? It seems only fair, given that we're picking up all this trash."

Louise didn't point out that the woman had yet to pick up a single scrap of paper.

"I think we should give it to Jack. Our workers may find other nice things. Maybe we can put a little notice in the paper and see if anyone comes forward."

"I don't think that's very likely, do you? I mean, I don't care. It's not something I would wear, even though it may be real gold. It's such fun to find lost treasure, though. My brother found a woman's fur neckpiece when he was little. One of those things with real fox heads, only beads for the eyes. My mother reported it to the police, but no one ever claimed it, so he got to keep it. I wonder what he did with it. It's not something that's politically correct to wear today, but it must have had some value then. He was good at spotting things. One summer he worked at a gravel pit for the highway department. He found a dinosaur tooth, at least that's what he said it was. It looked all chalky to me. Wonder where that is? Isn't it funny how you remember things? I haven't thought about that for ages. Maybe he donated it to a museum or something. I guess that would be the right thing to do. It would be quite a conversation piece on a coffee table, though."

"It's your turn to pick up, Dorothy."

"Just call me Dort. All my friends do. Here, I'll take the stick. I do want to do my share. I always taught my children ..."

Louise tried to block her partner's ongoing narrative by imagining a favorite symphony playing. Instead she kept hearing Salty's loud bass voice singing "He's a Doughboy from Ohio."

She couldn't fault Dort for not making a good effort, but her partner was easily distracted. She liked to pick up odd objects and discuss them, and it was surprising what had accumulated along the road over the winter.

"Look, one red tennis shoe." Dort dangled it from the end of her pick. "I don't see the other. How could someone lose a single shoe? If it was lost from a car window, wouldn't you think that they would come back for it?"

Louise couldn't understand why anyone would use the roadside as a garbage dump, but Dort didn't give her a chance to comment.

"I can just see kids out for a spin, throwing the shoe out the window to tease someone. It's big enough to fit a teenage boy."

The distance between them and the team ahead kept getting longer. If they didn't step up their pace, the pair following them would catch up. Louise was glad when it was her turn to do the picking. She was so intent on hurrying that she stepped into a patch of dried burrs before she realized it.

Her overalls were a magnet for the prickly little devils. She could feel them scratching through her stockings and bent to remove them. Because the burrs were old and dry, they broke apart when she tried to detach them, forcing her to pick at the remnants.

She and her partner were falling even farther behind.

Louise suggested that the person using the stick carry her own bag, and the other hunt for cans and bottles. Dort was agreeable about the way they worked—when she stopped talking long enough to hear suggestions.

Cans were easy to gather, apart from having to shake out some strange contents including a particularly bulbous spider, but bottles were more hazardous. Many were broken, and picking up shards of glass required caution. When Louise found an undamaged one, Dort was quick to react.

"Oh, that looks just like the old fashioned ones that used to hold my favorite drink, grape soda. Let me see it. It may be collectible."

Louise was weary of the job and didn't care if Tiffany's had made the bottle, but she held it up for her partner's inspection.

She nearly dropped it when a horn blared out. She looked up to see Florence crawling by in her car, heading toward Acorn Hill. She held her arm out of the window, as though toasting Louise with an imaginary bottle of her own.

Dort sputtered indignantly. "That woman nearly made me spill my garbage bag. The nerve of her, honking at us like that. I've seen her at the chapel. Isn't she married to that nice man who drove the van for us? Well, I'd like to give her a piece of my mind. If she can't be bothered to help, the least she could do is not flaunt her freedom when we're working so hard."

Louise chose to take Florence's gesture as a friendly greeting, even though it was annoying to be blasted by a horn. She started to drop the bottle into an orange bag, when Dort stopped her.

"I think I'll take that home with me, just for sentimental reasons. If it is an old grape soda bottle, it would look nice with some dried flowers in it. I do my own arrangements. I try to use things from the garden, although it's always tempting to load up at the craft store in Potterston. I hate to see a week go by without a visit for fresh supplies. I won't say that I'm an artist, but I do like to change the decorative items in my home with the seasons. I was noted for the wreaths I made when the ladies' guild at our former church had a bazaar."

By the time Jack came to pick up their first full garbage bag, Louise had new appreciation for working on projects with Florence. She could be a bit strong-willed, but at least she took time to breathe between commands and comments.

At noon the whole group went into Potterston for lunch at a fast food restaurant. Louise wasn't comfortable going to a public place in her pedal pushers and ruined hose, but the prospect of sitting in a booth was wonderful. Rev. Thompson had arranged to treat them from his discretionary fund, so everyone was encouraged to select whatever he or she liked. Louise ordered a salad and tea at the counter, then looked around, hoping to join Byrdie or Justine.

"Louise, there's an empty booth here," Dort called out, cutting off her attempt to find other company. "I saved it for the two of us. I do hate to be crowded when I eat. How much longer do you think we'll work? I signed up for the day, of course, but it's turned out to be harder work than I expected. I feel downright winded."

That Louise could believe.

Jane loved her aunt. Some of her fondest childhood memories came from trips to the Buckley farm. When Ethel had been persuaded to move into the carriage house, Jane had supported the idea wholeheartedly. In fact, she sincerely wished that Ethel would come home from her visit. It was the only way Jane was going to get off the kitchen phone.

"Oh dear, I've chatted quite awhile," Ethel said. "But I know you're laid up with nothing to do. There's nothing worse than being bored, I always say."

"I'm managing to keep busy," Jane said without much

conviction, moving the phone to her other ear. Her neck was getting stiff from holding the phone without hands, as she browsed through a cookbook while she talked.

"Did I tell you that I had lunch with an old friend from primary school?" Ethel asked.

She had, at least twice before, but Jane tried to be patient and hear the whole recitation again. Her aunt would never dream of passing the time of day for over an hour when Jane was working around the inn. She genuinely seemed to believe that she was doing a good thing by entertaining her invalid niece.

The sad thing was that Jane didn't have anything pressing to occupy her time. Salty had sweetly but firmly shooed her out of the kitchen so many times that it felt like alien territory. Alice was managing the inn with stoic determination, making decisions on her own without consulting her sisters. Jane knew it wasn't her usual way of doing things, but Alice felt pressured by new responsibilities.

"That's nice," Jane said into the phone. She hadn't been listening but hoped it was the right response.

"Are you girls eating good dinners?" Ethel asked with concern. "I know Louise and Alice will settle for sandwiches without you to cook for them."

"We're doing fine."

In fact, Louise was exerting herself to create a varied menu from her limited meal repertoire. She made substantial salads, presented in an attractive way. She defrosted some of Jane's soups and added prettily cut sandwiches. Alice offered hamburgers, broiled chops and steaks. After the first few meals, Jane knew both her sisters were becoming frustrated in their attempts to come up with different offerings. She told them that simple was fine, but suddenly began to crave a meal that included a flavorful sauce or a stir fry with the wonderful fresh asparagus that was now available or a homemade berry cobbler. She kept these cravings to herself. A mere suggestion of any of one of them would push her sisters over the edge.

She was aware that both of her sisters were taking on uncomfortable new responsibilities, however willingly they did so. What really made her feel bad was the highway project. Louise was being a wonderful sport, but it must be terribly distasteful for her fastidious sister to scoop up trash. She decided against telling her aunt about that.

"Now you take good care of yourself," Ethel said, at last breaking off the call. "If the doctor said to rest your leg for three weeks that means three. I know you. You're probably trying to walk on it already."

"I'm resting it," Jane assured her, not mentioning that she'd tried to walk and found it painful.

"The time will fly by. The older I get, the faster it goes. My son says it's because when you're ten, one year is a tenth of your life. When you're older, it's a fiftieth or a sixtieth, depending on your age."

"That's a good way to think of it." Jane still believed that two more weeks with crutches was an awfully long time. "I think someone just came in, Aunt Ethel. I'd better check. Thanks so much for calling me."

Jane rose from her chair and made her way to the hall door.

It wasn't a guest. Louise had come in looking worse for wear. Her short silver hair was so windblown it looked like a tattered halo, and her blouse had black smears on it. Her pedal pushers had a rip on the knee, and her hose were a mass of snags.

"Oh dear, are you all right?" Jane asked.

"Of course, I'm fine. I have to shower and change before my first lesson." She marched up the front stairs without another word.

A blast of sound assailed Jane from the parlor, and she hastened toward the library, her crutches thumping to the beat of "He's a Doughboy from Ohio."

❧

How could it only be four o'clock? Alice was sure her day had already been twenty-four hours long. It had taken forever to register a family staying at the inn for a rehearsal dinner tomorrow and a wedding at the Methodist Church Saturday. They were the groom's parents and his two younger sisters, and to say that they were excited was an understatement.

The younger girl, still in her early teens, was a bridesmaid, and she was bubbling over with details of the event. Perhaps because she'd exhausted her own family, she attached herself to Alice and related every tiny detail of the wedding plans. She was a sweet child, but she distracted Alice from all the things that needed to be done, including making dinner since Louise had lessons until six o'clock.

She was finally on her way down the stairs after showing the family to their rooms when Emily clearly called out to her.

"Do you have a minute, Alice?"

"Yes, of course. Come down to the kitchen. I could do with a lemonade." Alice decided the rule about guests in the kitchen had been relaxed recently, so she didn't think it was a problem to have Emily join her.

"The thing is," Emily said as they sipped from bubbly glasses of cola, "Henry and I have decided to enjoy ourselves and not talk about our future for a few days. Henry really enjoyed meeting you, and we'd both like to get to know you better. We're going to an art show Saturday, and we'd like to have you come with us."

"I'm not sure about leaving the inn. We've been stretched thin since Jane's accident, but I'd love to."

"What would you love to do?" Louise asked, coming into

the kitchen and looking more like her usual composed self in a fresh skirt and blouse and with her hair neatly arranged.

"Emily just asked me to go to an art show Saturday, but I'm not sure I should."

"Of course, you should," her sister said with mock sternness. "If anyone deserves some time off, it's you. I can handle everything while you're gone. After all, I don't have lessons on the weekend, and I haven't any plans. It will be a treat to stay home after the day I've had."

"It's settled then," Emily said. "Can you be ready to leave around nine? We thought we would have lunch there. It's outdoors and there are supposed to be acres of booths including some that serve food."

"It sounds lovely. I'll be ready."

After Emily left, Alice realized she hadn't even asked where the show was being held. Was she that eager to get away for a day? She loved the inn, but a nice outing with pleasant people like Emily and Henry would give her a chance to relax and revive her spirits.

"Oh, I hear my first pupil," Louise said. "It's little Nina. I do hope she's practiced. I'm not in the mood for tears."

Alice turned her thoughts to dinner, checking the fridge and freezer for ideas. Her sisters deserved something besides sandwiches, but her mind was a blank today when it came to meal preparation. She'd just about decided to bake some potatoes and serve them with cheese and broccoli as toppings when there was a loud knock at the back door.

Before she could get there, the caller knocked again, making her wonder who was so impatient. She was more surprised than she should have been to see the bat man.

"Oh, I wasn't expecting you." She went blank on his name at first but managed to come up with it. "Mr. Van Dinkle."

"Had a little time before supper. Thought I'd put on that chimney guard."

"Yes, that would be fine." It occurred to her that now was

the time to ask how much it would cost, but he didn't give her a chance.

"Brought my own ladder." He looked up at the high roof. "Extension."

"Ah, do you need anything from me?" She couldn't imagine what, but it seemed like something Jane would say.

"Nope."

She went outside and watched him carry an awkward-looking aluminum ladder to the best position. Now that she was watching, the chimney seemed to be a scary distance from the ground. She knew what falling from that height could do to a person, and the idea of having someone up on their roof was discomforting, to say the least.

There was no reason to stay. The man obviously knew what he was doing. She said a silent prayer for his safety, but she couldn't make herself leave. He was walking on the rooftop, carefully approaching the chimney and measuring it. Then he went back to the ladder and scurried down with the agility of a monkey.

Going back up went slower. He had to carry a metal grate with several heavy tools hanging from a wide leather belt. Alice held her breath as he climbed with only one hand free. She knew how often workers in all trades ended up in the emergency room. Hardly a week went by without some-one needing care for an injured eye, a broken bone or a severe gash. These were men who wore hardhats and knew what they were about, but things happened when their jobs were inherently dangerous.

The bat man flitted across the roof like the creature who'd given him his name. If he had any fear of being up so high, he totally concealed it. Alice had never been aware of any height phobia in herself, but watching him made her uneasy. One slip could be a disaster.

She told herself to go inside and leave the man to do his job, but her feet were rooted to the spot. She could feel a pulse pounding in her head, and her palms were damp. It was her fault if something happened. She'd agreed to have the guard installed, but the likelihood of a wild creature taking up residence in the chimney seemed too remote for the risk he was taking. She wanted to call him down and tell him to forget it, but what if her voice put him off balance and caused him to fall?

She'd never dreamed home maintenance could be so nerve-wracking. Jane never complained about having to supervise repairmen. Alice frequently saw life and death emergencies at the hospital without panicking, so why did she feel so upset regarding the bat man's safety? Maybe it was because there was absolutely nothing she could do to help him if he fell.

After what seemed like ages but was probably only a few minutes, he came down.

"That'll do it," he said matter-of-factly, beginning the chore of removing his ladder.

"Thank you," Alice said weakly, grateful that he was through.

The problem of dinner seemed unimportant after Mr. Van Dinkle's departure. She decided to walk over to the general store to see what they had that could be prepared in a matter of minutes, maybe frozen macaroni and cheese or TV dinners. Desperate times called for desperate measures.

Chapter Ten

J ane waited in her kitchen with some misgivings while Salty finished his piano lesson. It was nice of their substitute chef to include her in the Friday shopping trip to Potterston, and it also relieved Alice of a task. Since her sister had to work at the hospital until three, she already had enough to do for one day.

It was Salty's shopping list that perplexed Jane. Why did he need haddock fillets and heavy cream for breakfast? Grated Parmesan was on the list, and there was a nearly full container in the fridge. He'd also included nutmeg, sweet basil and cayenne even though there was an adequate supply of each in the spice cabinet. She certainly didn't begrudge him any ingredients he might want, but she was puzzled.

She'd just finished adding a few items of her own to the list, groceries for weekend lunches and dinners, when Salty came into the kitchen.

"Ready to shove off, Janey?"

"Yes, I have my purse and the list right here. I am curious though. How are you going to use the haddock? Maybe you have a recipe I can add to my file," she said tactfully.

"Oh, the fillets aren't breakfast." His laughter boomed in the confines of the room. "I saw the empty TV dinner cartons in the trash. I can't have my favorite ladies eating cardboard entrées. After we shop, I'm going to fix baked haddock, Salty style. All you'll need to do is pop it in the oven half an hour before you want to eat."

"Salty, we can't ask you to fix our dinner. You're doing more than enough already. We'll get along fine, really. I think Alice and Lóuise actually like an occasional ready-to-eat meal."

"Nice people like the Howard sisters shouldn't have to eat meals that are only a step up from army food. Hope and I are going to a fish fry with some friends of hers, so I won't be fixing dinner for us. Cooking is never any trouble for me."

"It's beyond the call of duty." Jane was catching on to his naval-speak, but, of course, he wasn't going to be dissuaded by anything she said. She had a whole new sympathy for sailors who saw a destroyer bearing down on them.

"My pleasure, Janey."

"About these spices and the Parmesan—"

"I'm sure yours are fine, but I'm always more confident when I use my favorite brands."

If Salty was any more confident, they would have to rename the inn. The Good Ship Salty came to mind.

Jane went out the back door so she wouldn't have to contend with the front-porch steps and made her way to Salty's vehicle parked on the street. He was quick to open the door for her, even though she was quite accomplished with her crutches now. She would be able to breeze her way through the supermarket.

When they got to the store in Potterston, Salty had a different idea.

"Wait here," he said as he parked in the lot. "I'll be right back."

"Why?" Her hand was on the handle, ready to open the door.

"Just do what Captain Salty says," he said in a teasing voice. "I'll be right back."

She got out of the car anyway and was standing beside it when he returned with a contraption that she'd seen before in the store but never dreamed of using.

"Brought you this rolling cart," he said proudly.

"Oh, thank you, but I won't have any trouble going through the store on crutches." She looked at the combination rolling chair and grocery carrier that he'd brought for her. It was as large as a golf cart and twice as conspicuous.

"No need to risk slipping or something. Look, this has a motor and steering. You'll get a kick out of it." He pushed it so close that it blocked her way to the store.

"Salty, I'm not going to ride on that. I'm perfectly capable of getting through the store on crutches."

"Course you are, Janey, but the store management isn't going to like it if you take a spill hopping up and down their aisles. You know how much businesses worry about being sued. That's why they have this buggy."

"Really—"

"Put your purse here where you can keep an eye on it, but you'd better leave the crutches in the car."

Now she knew how it felt to be abducted by an alien. She was tempted to wait in the car while he did the shopping, but she really wanted to see what Salty was going to buy.

She planted herself on the relatively comfortable seat and tested a lever that activated it, then went forward full speed ahead. It moved slightly faster than a child's tricycle, but it had a tendency to veer to the left. The average five-year-old would have a ball wheeling around the parking lot on it, but Jane felt like she was using it under false pretenses. What if someone who really needed it came to shop? She didn't want to deprive another person of its use.

"I really can't ride on this," she said.

"Sure you can, Janey. Here, I'll give you a push."

His manual override easily took control, and she found herself being propelled toward the entrance at a considerably faster speed. The automatic door opened at their approach, and he whisked her inside, still protesting.

The basket on the cart wasn't large enough for everything they needed, so he grabbed a cart for himself, leaving Jane to steer the big conveyance on her own. It veered to the left and bumped into a full load of groceries being pushed out by a woman in sweatpants.

"Watch where you're—" She looked at Jane and her face softened. "Oh, sorry, honey. Didn't mean to get in your way."

"No, it was my fault," Jane said, but the woman was hurrying toward the next aisle.

"This thing doesn't steer right," she hissed at Salty.

"You're not likely to do much damage going less than a mile an hour," he said with a laugh that caused several people to look in their direction.

Jane quickly learned two things about shopping while sitting in a motorized cart. First, she couldn't reach ninety percent of the things she wanted. Of course, Salty was in charge, so it didn't really matter on this trip. But what would she do if she were on her own? Could she stop strangers and ask them to hand her every item she needed?

Second, people didn't look at her. They didn't react with the usual casual glance of indifference of strangers who were absorbed in their own business. Instead, they pointedly ignored her. Their eyes automatically turned away. She was the invisible woman. She was different, not one of them anymore. It was a phenomenon that gave her a lot to think about. How did handicapped people want to be treated? She was the most conspicuous person in the store, and everyone pretended she wasn't there. .

She reached for a jar of olives that wasn't quite close enough. Rising up to grab it, she let go of the steering wheel for a moment, and the treacherous cart veered to the left where a cardboard display case of peanut butter blocked half the aisle. The cart crashed into it and jars fell everywhere.

Peanut butter with jelly, chunky peanut butter and smooth creamy peanut butter scattered across the aisle, immediately creating a logjam of shoppers with their carts.

Salty looked back, rapidly assessed the problem, ditched his own cart and came to the rescue. He righted the cardboard display with a few very seamanlike words and pushed Jane through the peanut-butter blockade.

She slumped down, as though that would make her and the ungainly cart disappear from sight. When Salty found the manager to complain about the faulty steering and the foolishness of blocking an already narrow aisle, she was ready to bolt. A little leg pain was nothing compared to the humiliation of having caused such a big commotion.

The manager's abject apology only made her feel worse. He assigned one of the baggers to be her personal shopping assistant as long as she was there. They were now a caravan with Salty leading the way and a gangly, inarticulate boy pushing her. She didn't know if she would ever have enough nerve to return to this supermarket.

That was when Salty started whistling. She'd heard him do it as he worked in the kitchen, but it seemed louder in the store. They finished selecting their groceries to the tune of "He's a Doughboy from Ohio."

Louise debated with herself whether to leave the inn unattended. Alice was working and Jane was shopping, but they weren't expecting any new guests until after the weekend. For now, they had that charming lady, Emily Cleary; the wedding party; and, of course, Bert Frame. At the moment, all was quiet.

She checked her image in the mirror over the bathroom sink and decided that hers was an urgent case. Since working along the highway, her hair had a mind of its own. She tried brushing it into submission, but several silvery strands refused to go where they belonged. It was imperative that she keep the hair appointment—and only fair—because she'd made it nearly six weeks ago after her last haircut.

Clip 'n' Curl was only a ten-minute walk, so she set off at a brisk pace, hoping Betty, the owner, would be able to take her on time. She was probably worrying for nothing, but she couldn't shake a sense of urgency about getting back to the inn as soon as possible.

Walking into the familiar little salon, Louise recoiled at the strong smell of perm solution. She was grateful that her simple wash-and-wear style spared her the long ordeal of getting a permanent wave. The downside was that it had to be trimmed at regular intervals.

"I'm running a little behind, Louise," Betty's friendly voice called out from beside the sink where she was removing a seemingly endless number of tiny curlers from the head of a woman Louise didn't know. "My new assistant up and quit with no notice, so I'm having to do double duty. I tell you, it's hard to get good help these days. I'll get to you as soon as I can."

"That's fine, Betty," she said, speaking loudly to be heard over the country music that played continuously in the shop.

She was tempted not to wait, but it wasn't likely that she could get a new appointment for tomorrow. Betty was usually booked solid on Saturday, especially during wedding season. Even if Betty wasn't preparing the bride and her attendants, which she often did, she would be rushed to style some of the guests.

Louise wandered over to the shelf where Betty kept magazines and sorted through the pile. There were several hair-styling issues, well-thumbed by customers looking for ideas on how to change their hairdos. The rest were mostly celebrity gossip magazines, the kind that were filled with articles about the fitness of movie stars or politicians. If the blurbs on the covers were any indication, readers were obsessed with every pound that the famous gained or lost.

She put aside the stack without choosing a magazine to read and sat on one of the cracked leather chairs in the waiting area. Huge posters of hair models filled three walls, and Louise mused that it must be extremely tedious to pose for a living. Imagine having nothing to do all day but get pretty, then sit for a camera. She was having a hard time sitting still while Betty finished the perm.

Of course, everything would be fine at the inn. Jane would be home before too long, and as far as Louise knew, all the guests were out for the day.

Betty was still removing curlers, obviously hurrying as much as she could. She was uncharacteristically silent as she worked. Perms certainly required a lot of rinsing. Whenever Louise thought that Betty surely must be done, she began another step.

Becoming hopeful when the customer moved from the sink to one of the chairs, Louise soon realized that her optimism was unfounded. The woman had a long, thick mane that Betty was styling with a hand dryer, seemingly one hair at a time.

Louise's patience was stretched thin, and she was sorely tempted to leave. But if she did, her waiting time would be wasted. How much longer could it take?

At last Betty was finished. The customer was tall and young with enough hair for two or three women. It fell to midback in a mass of dark brown curls. It was probably fashionable, but Louise would hate to comb the snarls from those curly locks.

"Sorry you had to wait, Louise," Betty said as she gestured for Louise to sit beside the sink for her shampoo.

"No problem. I haven't anything urgent to attend to." Louise hoped that her statement was accurate.

When she was done, Louise walked home lost in thought. She wasn't proud of her impatience at the beauty salon, and she was reminded of the Old Testament story of Job, a man who never lost faith in the face of the most horrendous setbacks. She couldn't hope to have the patience of Job, but she did need to pray about her role in the family. She wanted to be more understanding of her sisters' responsibilities and accept her own unaccustomed duties with love, forbearance and greater patience.

Her spirit was renewed by her quiet contemplation of Job's suffering and steadfastness. She silently prayed for Jane's healing and thanked the Lord for Alice's unwavering love and concern. Buoyed up by faith, she felt ready for whatever the rest of the day brought.

She hadn't expected a fire engine.

The huge yellow-green vehicle used by the volunteer fire department was parked directly in front of the inn. Two teenagers stood next to their bicycles, watching to see what emergency might be unfolding. She frantically looked at the house, expecting to see smoke curling from the roof or flames shooting from the windows. There was no sign of a blaze, but it was a large house. She rushed around to the rear, vaguely remembering that the kitchen was the room most vulnerable. But how could a fire start when no one was cooking?

Candles! Jane loved to burn them as air fresheners. No, she couldn't believe her sister would be so careless as to leave the inn without extinguishing even the smallest flame.

She circled the house without seeing any sign of a fire, although there was a slight smoky smell in the air. She saw an auxiliary fire vehicle pass the engine and continue slowly up Chapel Road, its red emergency lights flashing. Whatever was happening inside, she had to know. She instinctively took a deep breath and hurried through the front door.

"You're one of the owners, right?"

A tall fire fighter in full gear met her in the foyer. He was wearing a heavy-looking yellow coat, dark, rubbery pants, massive boots and a helmet. When she got past the shock of seeing him in full fire-fighting garb, she recognized him, although she didn't know his name.

"Yes. I'm Louise Smith. What on earth is wrong?"

"We got a call about a possible fire here. Please don't be alarmed. We're still checking, but it doesn't look like there is one. We have a vehicle cruising the area in case the fire is actually someplace else."

She had so many questions, she practically stammered in her haste to ask them.

"Who . . . who called? How could there be a fire? Wouldn't you know right away if there was one?"

"Not necessarily," the firefighter said patiently. "In a house this old, we have to check the walls to be sure there isn't an electrical fire. One of my men is in the attic, just to be sure everything is okay up there. We can't leave until we've gone over the whole place."

Louise looked beyond him toward the kitchen and saw Bert Frame hovering in the doorway. "Mr. Frame, did you call the fire department?"

"I called 911," he said sheepishly.

"But why?" She was almost afraid to hear his answer.

"I was using a computer in my room." He stuffed his hands into his pants pockets and seemed to shrink into himself under her gaze. "The power went off, and I smelled something burning. It seemed like the thing to do."

"I've got a pretty good sniffer," the fireman said, "and I haven't smelled anything inside the house, but we take it seriously when someone says they smell smoke."

"Yes, as I'm sure you should."

"Better safe than sorry. Now if you'll excuse me, ma'am, I've got a few more places to check."

"I'm grateful for your thoroughness," Louise said. "Thank you so much."

He went up the stairs, leaving her alone with the troublesome guest.

"I'm really sorry, Mrs. Smith."

"You did the right thing," she said wearily, remembering her own resolve to be more patient. "We're very conscious of fire safety. We have to be, accommodating guests in a late-Victorian house. It's much better to have a false alarm than to ignore a potential fire."

"I found the fire," a taller, younger fire fighter said, coming in the front door. "A neighbor down Chapel Road was burning some brush to get his garden ready to plant. I guess the wind was blowing this way."

Louise sighed with relief, then realized that the little phone light on the registration desk was dark. She walked over to a wall switch and flicked it, discovering that the power was off.

"I'll have to check the box in the basement," she said, more to herself than the two men.

"I'll be happy to do that for you, ma'am. Two emergencies in one afternoon. I hope you like excitement."

The young man grinned and headed toward the cellar stairs, apparently pleased to have been called away from his regular job. She'd heard that the volunteer firemen took a great deal of pride in their work. They went away for professional training before being accepted, then held regular sessions to hone their fire-fighting skills. Big fires were rare in Acorn Hill, but the fire department was called out to the countryside from time to time, particularly for brush fires.

Louise was puzzled. They'd had the electricity updated before opening the inn. It was very unusual to have an outage. She looked at Bert Frame, trying to conceal her suspicions.

"Mr. Frame, exactly what were you doing in your room?"

"Using my computer. Listening to music. Oh, I was

heating some water for instant coffee. I always travel with a small plug-in pot. Some motels don't have them in the rooms."

"Is that all?"

"No." He had the grace to look embarrassed. "My wife always puts a travel iron in my suitcase. Says I attract wrinkles like a magnet attracts nails. Since I'm closing a deal Monday, I was heating it to press my pants."

Louise could visualize the maze of cords and appliances. The rooms weren't wired for that kind of use.

The phone light went on, and she heard the refrigerator humming in the kitchen. The fireman had solved that problem easily enough, but what on earth was she going to do about Bert Frame?

"I'm terribly sorry," he said. "I've been so caught up in this business deal that I've been preoccupied. What can I do to make up for all the trouble I've caused?"

She wanted to say that he should find someplace else to stay. First the bat, then the flood. Now he'd brought out the volunteer fire department for a false alarm, and he'd knocked out the inn's electricity. What would Jane say to him? Would she tell him to pack his bags? Would kindhearted Alice forgive him one more time?

Louise felt an inclination to ask him to leave, but she searched deep for the patience that she'd prayed for. His stay was coming to an end. He meant no harm, and her maternal instinct told her that he just didn't do well on his own. No doubt his wife had her hands full looking after him.

"Everything is fine here," the first fireman said, coming down the stairs with the man who had been checking the attic. "But I recommend that guests not use appliances in the rooms. It overloads the circuits and a faulty cord can start a fire for real."

"I agree," Louise said. "It's one of the rules of the inn."

She glanced at Mr. Frame. He looked absolutely miserable. What could she say or do that would be worse for him than the guilt that she could read on his face?

Patience was hard. Forgiveness was harder. Making a decision was no snap either. At least she knew that her sisters would back her, no matter what she decided about their errant guest.

"Mr. Frame," she said in the stern voice usually reserved for piano pupils who didn't practice, "I know it wasn't intentional, but you could have put yourself and others in danger."

"Yes, I understand. You want me to leave."

His shoulders slumped even more than usual. He took off his glasses and wiped them on the tail of his olive green dress shirt that hung outside his drab gray trousers. When he didn't put them back on, Louise had the alarming feeling that he was going to cry.

"No, I didn't say that. But if you stay, you can't use anything but your computer in the room. You must keep the screens in place at all times and check the faucets before you leave the room."

"I'll make myself a checklist. My wife does that for me at home," he said, looking a little less grim.

"I'll help you make it. And you must check off each item every time you leave."

"Gladly. And it will be good for me to get out and have my coffee at the Coffee Shop."

The third fireman joined the other two in the foyer, and Louise thanked them profusely for their rapid and thorough response to the call.

"We're just glad there wasn't a fire. This is a lovely home," the first firefighter said.

She walked them to the front door and watched as they drove away in their huge truck. The unusual visit had attracted spectators including some teenagers. They'd probably spotted the fire truck on their way home from school. A couple of them looked disappointed that they weren't seeing more action.

After the firemen had gone and Louise had answered a few questions from concerned townspeople, she found a pad of paper at the registration desk and wrote out a short list of things that Bert had to do every time he left the inn. It felt as if she was writing out a lesson plan for one of her students as he dutifully waited for it.

When she was finally alone, she made herself a cup of herbal tea and sat at the kitchen table trying to decide how to tell her sisters about the latest adventure of Mr. Frame. Had she been too lenient in letting him stay after this last incident? She'd had to weigh compassion for him against the safety of the other guests. Now it was her responsibility to check on him until the moment he left.

Jane must have been making decisions like this every day, but Louise realized that she rarely was called upon to act as chief executive. It would be a relief when she could go back to her accustomed routine, handling the inn's finances and giving music lessons.

How was Jane doing with the books? Louise had been too busy to ask. More because she missed doing them herself than to check on her sister, she carried her tea to the library and sat at her father's big desk.

The account book was in the drawer where Jane had placed it, along with the checkbook and the bills that needed to be paid. She took them out, surprised to see the electric bill on the top of a rather substantial pile. It was nearly the end of May, and it seemed that Jane had yet to pay it.

Louise thumbed through the envelopes, each one an account that was due. A bit disturbed, she checked the ledger. Her own entry was the last one in it. Jane hadn't started to record expenses or income.

Louise couldn't have been more surprised if Wendell had started barking like a dog. With so much time on her hands, Jane hadn't even made note of last week's grocery purchases.

The simple solution was to catch up on everything herself. The house was quiet, and Jane might be away awhile longer since she and Salty had gone to the supermarket in Potterston. Louise's fingers itched to put everything right. If she hurried, she could get all their payments to the post office in time to go out this evening.

Much as she wanted to, she couldn't do it. Jane had agreed to take over the accounts. If Louise did them herself, it implied that she didn't trust her sister to take care of their finances.

She returned the book and unpaid bills to the drawer.

Chapter Eleven

Jane could hear Salty puttering in the kitchen after his Saturday piano lesson. He wasn't singing, whistling or humming as far as she could hear, and she knew what she should be doing in this quiet interlude.

The books and bills weren't going to take care of themselves. She wasn't usually a procrastinator, and it was inexcusable that she hadn't done a single thing with them so far.

First she had to set up her working space. She put a small bottle of water on a coaster and took out the accounting book. Once it was open to the appropriate page, she debated whether to pay bills first. The bundle had grown considerably since she took over the job, and she had yet to write a single check.

"Bills it is," she said aloud, trying to muster some enthusiasm for the task.

Before that, though, she had to select one of her father's fountain pens and fill it. She still had some pens in her room. Her pen and ink sketches were going much better than her accounting. The first pen she tried seemed too scratchy. It wouldn't do to rip through a check with a knife-sharp point. Her second choice was far too blunt. She couldn't possibly make neat figures like Louise's with such a clunky pen.

Her father's collection really was amazing. She picked up a red one that reminded her of tomato soup, recognizing it as an early form of plastic. There was another in yellow-orange and a third in mottled green. They were colorful enough to frame, and she toyed with the idea of doing just that. One of her favorites was sterling silver rendered in a gothic design, and she wondered whether some of them should be kept in a safe deposit box at the bank. She picked up a teal-blue pen with a matching mechanical pencil and noticed that they were embellished with genuine gold. Her father had always been excited to find a set in the original box.

She understood that her father's fascination with pens had little to do with their monetary value. He found them in places like thrift shops and tag sales, often buying them without knowing what their real value was. To him, it was all about the pleasure of writing his sermons in a fine script with handsome precision instruments.

Jane made a few lines on a piece of scrap paper and understood exactly why he'd collected them. No modern ballpoint could replicate the graceful swirls and inky beauty made possible by a fountain pen. And unlike earlier quills and pens that had to be dipped in an inkwell, they didn't leave unwanted marks or splatters.

She finally chose a rather simple model in black with a gold clip and gold trim. It had a pleasing Art Deco look about it in spite of being one of the plainer ones. She made a few strokes on the scrap paper and decided the lines were just right, not too fine or too thick. She felt ready to tackle the job.

"Excuse me."

She looked up to see one of their guests standing in the open doorway.

"Good morning, Mr. Frame. Is there something I can do for you?"

"Oh no, nothing. I guess you heard about the fire department."

Jane wanted to point out that the whole town knew about the false alarm at Grace Chapel Inn, but there was no point in being mean about it. Louise had made the decision to let him stay, and Jane felt obliged to back her up.

"Well, that's in the past," Jane said.

"I wanted you to have these."

He brought one arm out from behind his back and held out a large bouquet covered in green florist's paper.

"I know they don't begin to make up for all the trouble I've caused," he said, wrinkling his nose to push up his glasses. "But I wanted to say how sorry I am."

He came into the room and handed her the bouquet.

"How nice of you," she said, carefully removing the paper. "Thank you very much."

The flowers were really stunning, a dozen red roses artfully arranged in baby's breath and greenery. Most were only beginning to open, and Jane looked forward to many days of pleasure from the lovely blooms.

"I hope you like roses," he said shyly.

"How could anyone not like them?" she said with feeling. "It really was very thoughtful of you. I think I'll put them in the foyer where all of us can enjoy them, our guests too."

"Oh no, these are just for you. I got a plant for the hallway—mums or something. I'm not too good on flowers. And a bouquet for each of your sisters."

"Oh, that's really too much," she protested, rather stunned by the outpouring of flowers.

"Not at all. Your hospitality has been a big help in getting through some really tedious negotiations. I'm an accountant at heart, so handling the whole deal has been stressful, to say the least."

"You're an accountant?"

Jane looked at him with new respect. Anyone who could balance books was a wizard in her eyes.

"I'll be moving along now, Janey," Salty said, coming up behind Mr. Frame. "Say, what do you have here?"

"Roses from Mr. Frame," Jane said.

"Nice. Want me to put them in water for you?"

"I don't want to hold you up," Jane said.

"I'm not in a rush. I promised Hope I'd hang some new curtains in her living room. Not my favorite job, to tell the truth. I noticed a shelf of vases in the storage room. That green glass one would be my choice. Not showy enough to distract from the flowers but a good color."

Jane didn't want to admit it, but that was exactly the vase she would have chosen.

Salty took the flowers and promised to return them pronto, then glanced at the array of things on the desk.

"Getting at the books, are you, Janey? The paperwork in the navy was what did me in. I'd rather walk over broken glass than figure out my own taxes."

"I guess we're kindred souls then," she said with a forced laugh. "I am helpless where accounting is concerned. I've been putting it off all week."

"What do you have to do?" Bert asked as Salty took the flowers to the kitchen.

"Enter purchases and receipts, pay the bills, just routine stuff. I don't know why I've delayed getting at it."

"My wife is the same way," Bert said. "She looks at a stack of bills as if they were a nest of snakes. Is there anything I can do to help?"

"Oh, I couldn't ask you to do my work." Her protest sounded weak in her own ears.

"Actually, I've got time on my hands this weekend. There's nothing I have to do until we close Monday. If there's any chore I can do for you around here, I'll be glad to help."

The thought of setting Bert Frame loose to tackle any of

the inn's chores made her cringe, but bookkeeping was another thing. He knew how to do that. He must be good if his company trusted him on a big land purchase.

No, she couldn't ask a guest to do her work. Could she?

"Maybe I could sort of assist you. Walk you through any problems you might have," he said in a diplomatic voice.

"I suppose that would be all right. Yes, thank you, Bert. That would be really helpful."

If he were there watching, she absolutely would have to buckle down and get the job done.

They settled in on either side of the desk, Bert agreeing to sort a haphazard bundle of receipts while she started paying the bills.

Salty returned with the flowers and put them in a prominent place on the coffee table. He didn't say anything, and Jane hardly noticed that he was whistling his favorite tune as he left.

"Oh dear," Jane said, staring at a check she'd just managed to ruin. "I wrote eighty-nine dollars instead of ninety-eight. My mind wanders whenever I work with numbers. You must think I'm an idiot."

"Half the world seems to feel that way about numbers," Bert said soothingly. "Good thing they do, or what would geeks like me do for a living? Tell you what, I'll make out the checks and you can sign them. We'll polish them off in good order."

Louise looked in on them as they were beginning to record entries in the account book, Jane reading them aloud while Bert did the writing. If Louise was surprised or upset to see their maverick guest at work on the inn's finances, she didn't show it. In fact, she silently retreated, leaving Jane with her new and very efficient helper.

At first Alice was afraid that she would be a third wheel on the excursion to the art show. Henry and Emily were close, and their time together was limited and precious. But as they drove there, her doubts about joining them were soon dispelled. By the time they reached New Hedrick, they were visiting like longtime friends.

New Hedrick was in the heart of Pennsylvania Dutch country, and Emily, who had lived near an Amish community as a young child, was fascinated by the black buggies they passed on the way to the show.

"When I was little, we lived in Centerdale, Michigan," she explained. "Quite a few of the farmers in the county were Amish. They lived the way people had a hundred years earlier. We had our eggs delivered by an old man who drove a horse-drawn buggy just like the ones here. He came once a week, and I couldn't wait for his visit. Sometimes he even let me sit inside the buggy for a minute. I wonder if anyone took over his business when he got too old to do it."

"I remember two Amish brothers, Frederick and William, who worked at our hospital," Alice said. "They were young, still in their teens, but I've never seen more diligent workers. When they finished their shifts at the hospital, they both went to second jobs. They were saving up to get married and have their own farm someday."

"We moved from Centerdale when I was in the second grade, but I remember Loia Miller, the Amish girl who came to our house to clean once a week. She was young," Emily said, "probably only sixteen. The children all put their books on the teacher's desk and left school as soon as it was legal in Michigan. They liked to have a job before they were old enough to get married. Since we had little industry in our town, it was hard to find work. The girls who couldn't get a job at some small business would do housework. Mother loved having her come to do the ironing and cleaning. It gave her a chance to get out for a few hours too. My two sisters were both younger than I, so a trip to the hairdresser or a visit with a friend was a treat for Mom."

"Your dad worked for the state then, didn't he?" Henry asked.

"Yes, in the agricultural extension program. We moved to East Lansing when he started teaching at Michigan State. I really missed our little town at first. Once Loia took me to her family's farm to spend the day."

"Did you go by buggy?" Alice asked.

"No, in my parents' car. Mom or Dad would pick Loia up in the morning and take her home at the end of the day. The Amish in Michigan weren't prohibited from riding in cars, only owning them."

"I can understand that," Alice said. "I had some interesting conversations with our Amish boys. The way they explained it to me, it isn't that modern vehicles or electricity are bad. It's only that they encourage worldliness and dependence on outsiders. In fact, they told me that their mother had a kerosene-powered refrigerator, and their father used a generator for some outside jobs. They could use batteries too, but not the electricity generated outside the community."

"I remember being surprised that Loia didn't have a telephone at her house," Emily said. "Especially since she always talked on ours whenever she took a break from her work. It made me crazy because I couldn't understand a word she said. She talked in German to friends working at other houses."

"I do know one thing about the Pennsylvania Dutch, although I haven't had any personal contacts," Henry said, driving slowly through the town as he followed signs giving directions to the community center. "They were originally German or Swiss-German. The name came from *Deitsch*, meaning German."

"Henry loves history. I bet he can tell us the when, why and where of their coming here."

He laughed. "Most came from Germany, although some originally lived in Switzerland. As to why, European wars and religious persecution were the main reasons. They started coming before 1800." He stopped and turned to Emily. "Tell us more about the farm you visited."

"Well, if you insist." She smiled at her companion. "The inside of the house seemed dim to me at the time. I could hardly believe that people actually lived without electric lights. Loia's mother made a cake, and they let me help decorate it with lots of frosting, then take it home with me. I was disappointed, though. It had a funny taste, although I was polite enough never to mention it to Loia. Mom said it tasted different because it had been baked in a wood or coal stove."

"You were visiting strange and exotic places before you got out of elementary school," Henry teased.

Emily agreed, laughing. "I remember their barn. It seemed huge at the time, and I suppose they had ten or twelve horses. I was dying to ride one, but Loia said they were for work, not play. It's the rabbits I remember best, though."

"Why rabbits?" Alice asked.

"They had stacks of pens behind their house. I thought rabbits were supposed to be pets, so I was shocked to learn that the family used canned rabbit meat in the winter."

"I never thought of Michigan as Amish country," Alice mused.

"We were near the Indiana border. There were large Amish communities there."

"In fact, you'll find them in Maryland, Virginia, North Carolina, Ohio, West Virginia, Illinois, Iowa and more states than I can remember. I think they went as far west as Missouri and Nebraska, not to mention north to Ontario," Henry said as he made a right turn. "Start watching for a parking place. That seems to be the community center up ahead."

"Well, in spite of the rabbits, I did love Loia. She wore such different clothes, always plain colored cotton with a big white apron and a cap covering her hair. And she didn't use buttons. The front of her dress was held together by straight pins. I used to worry that she would prick herself."

"Buttons are associated with the military. So are mustaches, since soldiers used to be proud of big droopy ones," Henry said, spotting a parking space. "They were also signs of pride and individualism, no-no's for the Pennsylvania Dutch. At least the men don't have a problem deciding what to wear to work. Black trousers, black vest, black jacket, a straw hat in summer, felt in winter. My life should be so simple."

"When I was a child, I thought the men were jolly," Emily said. "They seemed to laugh a lot and enjoy life even though they worked hard. I wasn't so sure about the women. Loia's mother seemed really old to me, although she probably wasn't much over forty. I would hate to run a household the way she did. But then, baking and quilting aren't my idea of fun, and they take great pride in both."

Henry pulled over to park beside the curb, and a black buggy with a sleek-looking chestnut horse passed them.

"They try to avoid being worldly, but they do seem to take pride in their horses," Henry said.

"That was a married man driving the buggy," Alice remarked. "The single men are clean-shaven."

"Imagine," Emily said, "a girl marries a handsome face, then doesn't ever see all of it again. I admire their religious convictions and their sense of community, but long wooly beards make my fingers itch for scissors."

"Good thing I remembered to shave this morning," Henry teased.

They walked down the road to the community building, and Alice saw that row after row of stalls were set up in a field behind the late Victorian red brick building. The grounds around the building were a community park with play equipment, grills and tables for picnics. They went inside first where a large room with a stage at one end was crowded with people browsing through four long aisles of booths. There was so much congestion that they quickly agreed to view the outside displays first.

"I had no idea it was such a big show," Alice said as they made their way outside.

"It came up on a Web site when I was looking for things to do while Emily was here," Henry said. "I know she loves folk art, and I thought this would be a place to see a lot of it."

"Henry has an eye for art himself," Emily said with a broad smile. "His collection of watercolor landscapes is a delight to see."

"I'm not much of a traveler," he explained a bit shyly. "So I like being surrounded by pictures of exotic places like Egypt and Arabia."

"I like the ones of the English countryside the best," Emily said. "As much traveling as I've done for my job, I've never been to Britain."

"It would be a great place for a honeymoon," Henry quietly suggested.

Emily didn't reply. Alice sensed that marriage was a forbidden topic today, and that Henry had transgressed by bringing it up.

They stopped at the first booth. A series of portable screens hung with rather large paintings of barns, cows and other country subjects. Alice thought they would look nice on a calendar, but Emily hardly glanced at them.

When they were far enough away from the artist, a lean, bearded man in paint-stained overalls, she whispered, "I've never warmed up to acrylics. They always seem a bit garish."

"I liked the little pink pigs." Alice hated to dismiss any artist's work without saying something good about it.

Emily's reaction to a table full of folksy dolls was much more positive.

"Look, cornhusk dolls. I love this one." She picked up a creature that could have been a boy-child in green patched pants and a shirt made of what appeared to be the stained and tattered remains of a dish cloth.

"It's a gnome," Emily said, holding it up for Henry's inspection.

"Is that what it is? I thought it was a scarecrow."

"Silly!" Emily said, laughing and returning it. "I'll definitely think about it," she said to a rail-thin woman in a long print dress, explaining that they'd only begun to look.

On the rare occasions when Alice went to any kind of show, she always felt that it was somehow impolite to leave without buying anything. Of course, most of the time she was with Jane, and she relied on her sister's good eye for art to select some modest purchase. Today she felt rather at sea, surrounded by pretty things and some that seemed like future white elephants.

"What kind of art do you like, Alice?" Henry asked while Emily studied a large display of paintings on pieces of barn siding and other used lumber.

"Oh, I'm not very arty. I like a pretty picture, flowers and such. But I mostly leave the decorating to my sister Jane."

Henry's attention went to the booth where Emily was making a purchase.

"Are you buying that?"

To his credit, he managed to keep his tone neutral. Emily was so smartly dressed, today in a blue pant suit with a flowered blouse, but her taste in art was mystifying. She was in the process of purchasing a jagged piece of wood with a big-eyed creature painted in bright red, yellow and purple. Alice was reminded of the kind of picture that a child would draw in kindergarten, only no teacher would let a youngster use such splintery wood.

"My first gnome of the day," she said with delight.

Alice thought gnomes were little figures that one put in a garden. She'd never known anyone who collected them, but then, Jane had told her about collectors who were crazy for bathing caps, plastic candy containers and prizes from cereal boxes.

Henry seemed amused but a bit puzzled too when Emily bought a little figurine made of something that looked like hardened clay. It was only an inch or so tall, but it cost more than the big splintery plaque.

"It's the smallest gnome I have," she explained. "Miniature-making is a very exacting art. You have no idea how much work went into crafting this little fellow."

Alice had to admit that the table full of miniature figures was fun, and she especially enjoyed the miniature food section, tiny objects that looked good enough to eat. She decided to buy a miniature cake decorated with delicate pink flowers for Jane's birthday. The seller added her sister's name using a small syringe filled with paint. She had no idea what Jane would do with the cake, but at least she'd participated in the show by buying something.

"You haven't bought anything," Emily chided Henry after they'd thoroughly covered the long outside rows. "Let's look inside."

"I have a better idea. If the food in that tent tastes half as good as people have told me, I'm all for an early lunch."

He led them toward a long white tent set up in a park area to the north of the community building. Visitors were already drifting toward the picnic tables that surrounded it. Judging by the growing line waiting beside the tent, the food was a big part of the show's attraction.

Alice saw that all the women working under the big tent were Pennsylvania Dutch. They bustled among an elaborate setup of portable stoves and serving tables. A menu was written in chalk on a freestanding blackboard, and a pink-cheeked matron in a dark blue dress, white apron and a cap that covered her hair was taking orders. Two young girls served as waitresses to deliver the food on plastic trays that looked like relics from a school cafeteria. They spoke to each other in German but were fluent in English when speaking to patrons.

"I can't decide," Emily said, reading through the rather long list of entrées. "I haven't had corn pie in ages, but sauerkraut dumplings are such a treat. Oh, they have hot potato salad. That's tempting too."

Alice shared her dilemma. This was unlike any tent meal she'd ever attended. There was an incredible choice considering that it was being served picnic-style. The women must have cooked all night to prepare so many special dishes. Alice was leaning toward chicken and dumplings, perhaps with spiced cabbage as a side.

"Tell you what," Henry said as they got closer to their turn. "Why don't we all order something different, then share? That way we can taste a lot of different things."

"Good idea," Emily said, and Alice quickly agreed.

Alice ordered the chicken-dumpling casserole, impressed that the woman taking their order didn't need to write anything down. She also added dandelion greens with hot bacon dressing and a generous piece of black walnut cake. Emily opted for the corn pie with fried sausages and sauerkraut dumplings, laughing at herself for ordering such a hefty lunch. Henry chose pork chops and sauerkraut with apple custard pie for dessert. He also got a funnel cake for them to share, tempted by the golden brown delicacy cooked in front of them in hot oil and sprinkled with powdered sugar.

They carried three heavily loaded trays to a log table on the fringe of the area, and Henry did the honors, dividing the food among them so they could sample all the luscious dishes. Alice was reminded of how she and Mark liked to order in restaurants, sharing so they could taste more items. They especially enjoyed fish platters that gave a sampling of many seafood entrées and appetizer trays with deep fried cheese sticks and zucchini. Sometimes it was awfully nice to have a partner.

"I can't believe how hard they must have worked to have so many good things ready for lunch," Emily said, taking a dainty bite of the funnel cake while it was still hot. "I saw a Pennsylvania Dutch cookbook for sale inside the community building. I'm trying to think of someone who would like it as a gift. There's no way I would ever spend so much time cooking."

"Fortunately, I love to cook," Henry said with a boyish grin.

They enjoyed their meal and the relaxed atmosphere of the dining area, but Alice felt a twinge of guilt at eating so much. When they were finished, there was a long waiting line at the tent, but the community building wasn't quite as crowded. There was a lot of art on display at the inside booths, and Alice's attention drifted as her companions discussed the merits of different watercolors in art terms beyond her understanding. Although she was having a nice time, enjoying Emily, Henry and the outing, she didn't have a very deep interest in what she was seeing. Jane, on the other hand, would have loved to be here. She would have come away from it with all kinds of ideas for her own art. Their lives certainly were topsy-turvy these days. She was spending the day with art, and poor Jane was stuck with bookkeeping.

When Emily bought a recipe book for a friend at work, Alice decided it was something Jane would enjoy too. She'd always been interested in Pennsylvania Dutch cookery.

Since she now had two gifts for Jane, she started looking for something Louise might like. The quilting displays caught her eye more than most, especially one where two Amish women were selling lovely hand-sewn comforters. They also had small items, and Alice bought a quilted bag with a lavender and blue diamond pattern. It would serve nicely to carry music when Louise played at church or elsewhere.

It also occurred to her that Salty deserved a little thank-you gift for all the work he was doing at the inn. She had no idea what to get, but Henry suggested a pair of potholders. "I'm always scorching mine," he said with a chuckle.

She selected a pair of nice thick quilted ones in red, white and blue that seemed appropriate for a former navy man. She also bought a few key holders for herself and friends at the hospital. They had two-by-two-inch quilted squares attached to a ring, making them easy to fish out of a purse.

It was midafternoon before they left, and Alice was hard-pressed to keep her eyes open on the ride home. She rested while Emily and Henry spoke softly in the front seat.

The day seemed to have been a success for them. Alice had enjoyed it, but she couldn't help wonder what it might have been like if she'd shared it with Mark.

Chapter Twelve

Jane never dreamed that she would create a commotion just by going to church. In fact, she was getting along so well on crutches that she didn't hesitate to walk to the chapel for the Sunday morning service.

"I could drive you," Louise had offered.

She declined with thanks. Getting in and out of the car would be more awkward than going there on her own power. Grace Chapel was, after all, only a hop, skip and a jump from the inn. She did compromise and agree to use the road rather than the convenient but rather uneven footpath that was their usual way of reaching it.

With a sister on either side, hovering protectively while pretending not to be watching her every step, Jane made her way to church. Walking outside seemed more strenuous than hopping around inside the inn, but she got there only faintly winded.

She'd hoped to sit in a pew near the front without attracting undue attention. Harvey Racklin gave her the first indication that it wouldn't happen.

"I'll get that door for you, Miss Howard." The usually grumpy retiree practically sprinted to reach it before either of her sisters could open it.

He did everything but spread a cloak before her as she self-consciously hobbled inside. Harvey was the last person she would have suspected of latent chivalrous impulses. Apparently her crutches had triggered his better side, since he rarely did more than grunt if she wished him good morning.

"Thank you, Harvey, and thanks for helping with the highway cleanup too. I've heard how hard everyone worked."

"Don't fall now," he warned. "Easy to do that on crutches."

"I'll be careful," she promised.

Louise made her way to the chapel's organ, and Alice talked softly with a friend. Jane started to go to her seat, but half the congregation seemed to converge on her before she could move forward.

"Jane, I'm so sorry about your injury," Vera Humbert said, hovering protectively by her side while her husband Fred added his consolation.

Several others asked how she was doing and expressed their sympathy. Naturally they were curious about how she'd been injured. She gave an abbreviated version several times.

She couldn't have gotten more attention if she'd been laid up for a year. Finally, when Louise began playing a prelude, Jane's well-wishers started drifting toward their places. Jane was poised to follow them when Florence Simpson materialized at her side.

"Jane, dear, I've been meaning to come check on you, but my life has been so hectic lately. I'm president of two groups this year, and you know how things come to a head in the spring, banquets and all. I promise I'll come by tomorrow."

"That's okay, Florence. I'm much better. I'll be back to normal soon."

The older woman adjusted her hat, a broad-brimmed ivory silk creation that matched the background color in a linen suit with thin navy stripes. Jane opened her mouth to express admiration for the outfit, knowing that Florence put a great deal of effort into her wardrobe, sometimes going into Philadelphia to shop the better stores. She also wanted to distract her from the topic of injuries in general.

Jane didn't have a chance. "You know, my cousin Bertha took a nasty fall down the front porch steps some time ago. Her back has never been the same. Are you sure you didn't hurt yours when you fell?"

"Yes, quite sure." Jane tried to move forward, but Florence had her wedged against the end of a rear pew.

"You should have your back X-rayed just to be sure," Florence went on. "I always say better safe than sorry. My cousin wore a back brace for the longest time, but it never seemed to help. Maybe you have a little twinge that you've ignored."

"My back is fine. Aren't you singing in the choir this morning?"

"No, my voice isn't quite up to par. Fortunately there's a soloist this morning, so I won't be greatly missed. Of course, I could do the solo part, but the choir director is trying to encourage our younger members."

"That's always a good idea," Jane agreed, not wanting to be late. "Church is going to start."

Jane started to move just as Florence stepped in front of her. The crutch came down wrong, and Florence yelped in pain.

"Oh, I'm so sorry!"

Jane grabbed the pew behind her for balance and stared in horror at Florence's contorted face. One rubber crutch tip had come down on the top of Florence's beige pump.

She kicked off the shoe and bent to massage her injured toes, moaning so loudly that several people in the nearby pews turned to look.

"Florence, what can I do? Are you badly hurt?"

"I certainly hope not," she said in the voice of a martyr. "No, don't you worry, Jane. I'll be fine. If you'll just get my husband. He's near the front. He'll help me to my place, and I'll go home after church and put some ice on it. I have a very high tolerance for pain."

Her groans seemed to belie that claim, and Jane felt horrible. She had been eager to get away from Florence, but she certainly hadn't wanted to hurt her.

"I'll get Ronald," she said, torn between feeling guilty and helpless.

"No, no, I've changed my mind. He'll only make a fuss, and you know how much I hate that. I'll just stand here a minute until the throbbing stops. I'd better put my shoe back on before my foot swells. Wouldn't want to attend the service with one on and one off."

The congregation stood to sing the opening hymn. Jane didn't know what to do. She felt responsible for Florence, but Alice would worry if she didn't come.

"Let me help you to your seat," she said, totally forgetting that she was stuck on crutches herself.

This was no time to think of herself. She put the crutches aside and took Florence's arm. It wouldn't hurt that much to go a few steps without them.

"Oh mercy, no! I can't have you walking without your crutches just to help me," Florence said with alarm. "What would people think? No, I'm quite capable of walking on my own."

She handed Jane the crutches with an authoritarian flounce, then limped ahead of her down the aisle.

Jane followed, trying not to see the turned heads and curious stares. Did she only imagine that the singing faltered as she passed each pew?

She fervently hoped that Rev. Thompson wasn't going to preach about healing the lame.

"What happened to you?" Alice whispered when the hymn was finished.

"I'll tell you later," Jane whispered.

Rev. Thompson's sermon was based on the parable of the sower, one of Jane's favorite Bible stories. He read from chapter thirteen of Matthew, telling how seeds planted in rocky places withered, and those planted among thorns were choked.

"'Still other seed fell on good soil, where it produced a crop—a hundred, sixty or thirty times what was sown'" (Matthew 13:8).

Jane thought of her own garden, which Alice had struggled to prepare for the plants that would bloom in glory all summer. She felt so blessed by the goodness in her life and especially for the sisters who had cared for her as a child and still nourished her with love.

In silent prayer, she asked for patience in dealing with Florence. In this honest moment with the Lord, she had to admit that she had been overly eager to get away from her. Sometimes Florence was a particularly hard person to love, but Jane promised to make amends by giving her the attention she craved.

When the service was over, she knew Alice was curious about the delay in joining her. She didn't have a chance to ask. Members of the congregation swarmed around Jane, showering her with attention that she neither wanted nor needed.

"Florence," she called out when she spotted her limping toward the door.

"I accidentally came down on Florence's toe with a crutch. I'm afraid it really hurts," she said, redirecting people's sympathy to the older woman. She was gratified that several women went over to see if Florence was okay.

"What was that all about?" Louise asked as they walked home.

"I was trying to get away from Florence, and I accidentally landed on her toe."

"Goodness, I hope you didn't break it," Alice said. "Do you think I should go to her house and check?"

"I imagine she would appreciate it. So would I."

Much as she hated giving Alice one more task, Jane knew that Florence would be pleased to have a nurse check on her at home.

"No broken toe," Alice said cheerfully when she returned from visiting Florence.

She sat down at the kitchen table, where Jane and Louise were having a light lunch that Salty had left for them.

"Thank the Lord," Jane said with feeling. "I feel so bad about hurting her."

"I suspect Ronald will suffer the most, since Florence seems to require constant attention. When I left, she was icing her foot while her husband fixed a luncheon tray for her. I checked her, but her toes didn't seem bruised. Maybe her shoe took most of the impact. I saw some heels with those fashionable pointy toes by the front door. I think your crutch mostly landed on empty shoe leather."

"Pointed toes look terribly uncomfortable to me, but I guess Florence's fashion sense saved her toes this time," Louise said.

"Maybe her feet hurt even before you came down on them," Alice said.

"I hope you're hungry," Louise said. "I've told Salty again and again that he doesn't need to fix meals for the three of us, but he seems to be having a great time acting as our chef. He hasn't had a chance to try many new recipes since he worked at an officers' club. It's hard to cook for just oneself."

"He made individual salads for us—baby spinach, red onion and tomato," Jane said, "and, of course, a Salty-special horseradish dressing. The man should write a cookbook. By the way, Alice, I had a chance to read a few recipes in the book you brought me. I can hardly wait to try some Pennsylvania Dutch cooking."

Louise took Alice's salad from the fridge, dribbled on a small amount of dressing and put it on the kitchen table.

"Homemade bread sticks," Jane said, pushing a platter toward her sister. "He made them with stone-ground flour. I've never had any quite like these, but I can't fault them."

"They're sort of chewy and nutty," Louise said, sitting and helping herself to another. "I like them even without butter."

This was Alice's favorite time of the week. The three of them tried to keep their schedules clear for a family meal on Sunday, even if it was only a salad luncheon. They relaxed and talked over the week's events, something that had been unusually hard to do after Jane's injury had plunged them all into new and unfamiliar tasks.

Today they particularly enjoyed the quiet meal. The guests from the wedding party had checked out, and they had only Emily Cleary and Bert Frame this evening. Next week promised to be another busy one, so this break was especially welcome.

They were finishing their cups of stewed rhubarb, which Louise had convinced Salty to make instead of rhubarb pie, when the phone interrupted their peaceful interlude.

"I do hope it's not a last-minute reservation," Louise said, getting up to answer it.

Alice agreed. They were expecting another fully booked week, and they all needed a bit of free time.

"It's for you," Louise said, handing the phone to Jane.

The conversation was brief, and Jane looked pleased when she hung up.

"Rev. Thompson is taking several members to an interchurch evangelism meeting in Potterston. He thought I might like to go along."

"I hope you agreed," Alice said. "It will be good for you to have an outing."

"Yes, he's picking me up in about forty-five minutes.

There's a dinner afterward, so I won't be home until this evening."

She made her way upstairs to freshen up, and Alice was glad that Jane had something to do.

"Well, it's just the two of us," Louise said. "I have to confess that some downtime is very appealing. I'd like to put up my feet and read some of my music magazines. I'm trying to find a way to interest little Nina in the piano. Her lessons aren't going well at all, but her mother insists that she continue."

"That's so hard for you," Alice said sympathetically. "I don't see how you can teach someone who doesn't want to learn."

"I haven't given up yet, but she is a challenge."

The phone rang again, and Alice was tempted not to answer it. But, of course, they were a business, and that would be highly unprofessional. She reluctantly picked it up.

"For you," she said, handing it to Louise.

"I did plan to . . ." her sister said after listening a moment.

"That's really nice of you, but . . ."

"Yes, I do have a soft spot for bluegrass music." She laughed softly.

"It seems I won't be catching up on my reading," she said, replacing the phone and smiling ironically.

"Oh?"

"That was Salty. He and Hope have tickets for a bluegrass concert, a fund-raiser for the Potterston food pantry. But Hope isn't feeling well, a spring cold or something. He doesn't want to go alone. There's really no reason why I shouldn't go. I'm meeting him at the high school auditorium a little after two so we can get good seats."

"You'll enjoy it," Alice said. "You deserve some entertainment. I'll clean up the kitchen."

After Louise left, the inn seemed unnaturally quiet. Even Wendell had disappeared, no doubt napping in one of his secret places. The cat knew cubbyholes where even the three sisters couldn't find him. Now that he was older, he was terribly self-sufficient. However, the tabby was still inclined to seek out one of the sisters for a little petting and purring or a tasty treat.

Alice knew that there were all kinds of chores that could be done, but she didn't feel motivated to begin anything. She went to the registration desk in the foyer, deciding to confirm that they were filled to capacity for the week. No cancellations had come yet, so it would seem that every room would be occupied. The thought made her feel a little weary.

She was startled when Bert Frame came bounding down the stairs with uncharacteristic energy.

"Is she here yet?" he asked, straightening a green-and-navy striped tie that actually went well with his somewhat crumpled suit.

"Who?"

"My wife. Of course, I see she isn't. Anna is never late. Probably my watch is fast. I sometimes set it a few minutes ahead so I get to my appointments on time."

"Your wife is coming here?"

"Oh, sorry, I forgot to ask whether it's all right for her to join me overnight."

"Of course it is." She wanted to ask how keeping his watch set ahead made any difference if he knew it was fast, but instead she just smiled.

There were three sharp raps on the front door, and Bert bounded toward it.

Alice had never visualized a wife for Bert, but Anna Frame would have surprised her if she had. She was as tall as or taller than her husband. Her dark brown hair was pulled back in a bun, accentuating high cheekbones and a rather sharp nose. Her lips were thin and colorless, and her tan pantsuit did nothing to enliven her face. Her eyes were another matter. They were slightly slanted and seemed unusually large, but the color was hard to define other than that they were lively and dark. Her hands seemed too large for her slender arms, and she was wearing rugged brown sandals with tan cotton socks.

Then she smiled at her husband, and her whole face was illuminated.

"Sweetheart, I want you to meet one of the wonderful ladies who've gotten me through this awful separation. Miss Howard, Alice, this is Anna." He beamed with pride.

"I'm pleased to meet you," Anna said. "I know how hopeless my husband is when he's preoccupied with work. You've been more than kind."

"Our pleasure," Alice said, feeling a bit awkward since they'd been tempted on more than one occasion to ask him to leave.

The Frames were polite, but they were so wrapped up in their reunion that Alice might not have existed. Bert and Anna seemed as much in love as newlyweds, although she vaguely remembered Bert mentioning a trip they took for their twentieth anniversary.

At least she could rest easy in the knowledge that Bert wouldn't be letting in wild creatures or flooding the inn while his wife was there to keep tabs on him.

Louise had had the right idea when she insisted that Sunday afternoon was a time for quiet pleasures. Chores could wait. Alice had a new mystery tucked away in her room for just such an opportunity, and it was warm enough to sit on the front porch to read. She started upstairs to get it and was surprised to see Emily coming out of her room.

"I didn't know you were here."

"Sorry if I startled you. I just came back to change."

She was wearing tan walking shorts and a white knit shirt, the first time Alice had seen her in any color but blue.

"I hope you're enjoying your stay," Alice said just to be saying something.

"Too much, I'm afraid." She looked more distressed than happy. "I'm having the most wonderful time with Henry. We're going to play tennis. I haven't had time for it in ages, but I used to love it. In fact, I was even on a team in college. Now I'll be lucky if I can hit the ball at all."

"I'm sure it will come back to you, like riding a bike."

"You're sweet to say so." Emily smiled but her eyes still looked sad. "Oh, Alice, I just don't know what to do. Henry and I have been keeping ourselves busy to avoid talking seriously about our future, but I have to make a decision soon. It's not fair to him to put it off, but I just don't know what to do. I love him dearly. He's the most wonderful man I've ever met, but I can't envision living in Potterston."

"It's quite a nice town, not large but not small like Acorn Hill." Alice didn't know what else to say, and Emily seemed to want input from her.

"It's a lovely place, but I don't know whether I can leave my job to be the wife Henry deserves. I suppose what I do is more a cause than it is just a job. Proper dental work can change lives, free people from pain, give children a chance of keeping their teeth in later years. I know I'm not a dentist, but I am a good fund-raiser and organizer. The need is so great." Her voice trailed off, and she looked even more unhappy.

"It's a terribly hard decision."

Alice wasn't thinking only of Emily. She and Mark had parted many years ago for reasons that reminded her of Emily's plight. In their case, different goals and priorities had led to the pain of separation. They still found it too difficult to give up their lifestyles to be together.

"I don't know what I'm going to do." Emily shook her head. "But I have to decide soon. I can't leave him hanging."

"No," Alice agreed, distressed because a person she had come to like was in such a predicament.

"Maybe if we'd met when we were younger, we could have had a traditional marriage. Things get harder when you're older and more set in your ways."

Alice didn't think a life-changing decision was ever easy, but nothing she could say would be helpful to Emily. She didn't know whether she regretted not marrying Mark all those years ago. Her life was full and satisfying. She loved her job, her family and especially the Lord. Would her commitment have been as strong if she'd joined her life to that of a man who, at the time, had not accepted her faith?

"Well, I have to go," Emily said with a smile that didn't mask her sadness. "I drove Henry's car to come back to change clothes. I have to meet him at the tennis courts in Potterston. The least I can do is not keep him waiting."

Alice continued up to her room on the third floor and found the book she'd been wanting to read. Soon she was settled on a lounge chair on the porch, but she quickly lost interest in the story unfolding on the pages of the novel. She didn't doze, as she sometimes did on a warm afternoon with no immediate demands on her time. There were too many thoughts dancing around in her head to fall asleep.

Was there anything she could have said to Emily to help with the decision? She didn't think so. Her renewed friendship with Mark meant a great deal to her, but she didn't honestly regret parting from him so long ago. He'd spent most of his career traveling to exotic places, searching out and treating the large animals that continued to fascinate him. Alice knew that she would have been superfluous in many ways, unable to share in his most important interests. Her own need to help others might never have been realized if she hadn't become a nurse, and, most importantly, his early rejection of religion would have driven a wedge between them.

She'd felt great joy for his sake when he accepted the Lord, but she also realized that her solitary path wasn't cause for regret. For a few minutes, when her sisters had left and even Bert Frame seemed to have a soul mate, she'd had moments of regret. It would be deeply satisfying to have Mark beside her at this moment when the inn was empty and she was by herself, but she knew that she was never truly alone. Jesus was with her every moment of every day, and the Lord would never forsake her.

Chapter Thirteen

Louise felt especially cheerful Monday morning. She looked out her bedroom window and saw that it was a sunny, if somewhat windy, morning that matched her mood.

The bluegrass concert had given her a lift, even though it wasn't something she would care to attend very often. Perhaps it was Salty's enthusiasm that had made it seem like such good fun.

Then she remembered.

Today was another highway-cleaning day. Jane had told her that she shouldn't feel obligated to take part, but Louise hated to back out. She'd signed on to help, and she wasn't going to let down the rest of the crew.

Jane once again lent her the pair of overalls that she used for gardening. For breakfast, though, she elected to go downstairs in a more conventional skirt and blouse.

On her way to the kitchen, she encountered Bert Frame in the foyer. He was with a tall woman in a mustard yellow pantsuit. She seemed unexceptional to Louise, but her first impression changed radically as soon as the woman smiled.

"Mrs. Smith," Bert said, "you didn't get a chance to meet my wife. Anna, this is the third lady who's done so much to get me through my bachelor stint. And believe me, dear, I hope you don't leave me on my own again very soon."

"So nice to meet you, Mrs. Frame. You're leaving now?" She noticed his bags and a neat plaid carry-all sitting on the floor.

"Yes, your sister Alice was kind enough to check us out last night," said Mr. Frame. "I have an early appointment in Potterston. Once that's over we're on the way home." He beamed with happiness.

"Well, I hope you have a good trip. If you ever come this way again, please keep us in mind."

It was the conventional thing she said to all departing guests, but Louise had her fingers crossed. Bert Frame was a sweet man in his own way, but she would breathe easier once he was gone. On his own, he was a disaster waiting to happen.

"Oh, Bert, you're ready to leave?" Jane came out of the kitchen, moving quickly on her crutches.

"On our way," he said with satisfaction.

"It was nice meeting you, Anna." Jane balanced on one crutch and offered her hand. "Bert helped me so much with the bookkeeping. I can't tell you how much I appreciate it. He made the whole process seem easy."

"He does have a way with numbers," his wife said.

When the Frames had left, Louise asked, "You had trouble with the bookkeeping?"

Jane shrugged. "I kept putting it off until I didn't know where to start. Actually, he walked me through the whole process and made it seem easier."

"You could have told me. I would have been glad to do it. I rather enjoy keeping the books and paying all our bills on time."

"No, I had to be responsible for it. You're doing so many extra jobs."

"It's only temporary. I'll take over the accounting this week."

"No, I can do it. Mostly I just needed more confidence.

Bert showed me a way to organize receipts and credit card slips that made it all much clearer. You have much too much on your plate right now."

Louise raised one eyebrow and gave her sister a skeptical look.

"Well, if you encounter any difficulty, let me know. I rather miss doing my bookwork."

"I will. Salty has breakfast ready for us," Jane said, "but I wish you would change your mind about picking up trash. I'm sure they can get along without you."

"No, I'm going," Louise said firmly. "What if all the workers decided that they weren't needed today? We can't leave Jack out there alone with an empty truck and no helpers."

"We have had a couple of people back out," Jane admitted. "Rachel has to leave on an antiques buying trip with her husband. She said they're really low on stock for the store, and their busy season is coming. Dorothy Gunnerson isn't coming either, although I'm not sure why. She gave me such a long explanation that I lost the thread of it. Something about fingernails and her great aunt's allergy to pine needles."

"Oh, she was my partner." Louise tried not to smile, but she felt better about the day's work. Dorothy had her good points, but it was difficult to concentrate on the job when she never stopped talking.

"The bad news is," Jane said hesitantly, "that you'll be partnered with Harvey Racklin, but he can be quite pleasant. Remember, yesterday at the chapel he held the door and asked how I was doing."

"If I recall correctly, he worked hard last time and didn't talk much. We'll get along fine."

"Of course, you will," Jane said with a little giggle. "Men always respect you."

"What do you mean?"

Instead of explaining, Jane turned on her crutches and

headed toward the kitchen. Louise wondered whether her sister was teasing because she'd gone to a concert with Salty. It was true that he'd become a friend, albeit an unusual one. She liked him quite well when he wasn't singing.

Louise enjoyed a fruit compote and an exceptionally tasty bacon quiche for breakfast, suspecting that Salty was trying to fortify her for the day of trash-removal.

"I'd come along to help you," he said, "but I promised to take Hope to some mall where manufacturers send leftover merchandise."

"An outlet mall, you mean. Is she feeling better?" Jane asked.

"I doubt it, but there's nothing like the smell of bargains to perk a woman up, is there?" He laughed at his own wit.

Soon after breakfast Louise made her way to the chapel parking lot where the work crew was assembling. Harvey Racklin was there ahead of her, and he only grunted when she mentioned that they would be partners for the day.

"Too windy," he said as they got into his car to drive to the spot on the other side of the road from where they'd left off last time.

Louise had to agree. She'd taken the precaution of putting on a heavy coat of sunscreen, but the wind promised to be the bigger problem. The sun kept ducking behind the increasing clouds, then reappearing.

"I didn't check the weather report," she said. "Is it supposed to rain?"

"They never know what they're talking about," Harvey said, dismissing twenty-first century meteorology with a single sentence and a sour expression.

Either Jack or Jane had done some recruiting because they'd picked up extra workers, who arrived in several vehicles soon after Harvey had parked his car. In fact, Jack predicted that they would be done before lunch. Louise hoped he was right.

"You hold the bag," Harvey said.

"I'll take the first turn, but we should switch jobs every fifteen minutes or so. That way it won't be quite as tedious."

He was wearing a green baseball cap that shaded his eyes, but the way he pursed his lips left no doubt about his opposition to that idea.

"We'll see."

That was like a student saying, "I'll practice if I have time."

Louise shook a plastic bag so hard it crackled and held it ready to receive litter.

"If you prefer, we can switch every time one of us fills a bag. Your choice."

"That's better," he grudgingly agreed. "Won't break the rhythm that way."

She didn't see anything rhythmic about gathering trash, but the matter was settled.

Harvey covered the ground assigned to them with an eagle eye, not overlooking the tiniest bit of paper. Louise certainly couldn't fault his work ethic, but his silence made the time drag. She didn't miss Dorothy's incessant chatter, but a person could be too quiet. She tried several times to start a conversation, but he only responded with vague noises.

"Do you think this is a project the church should be doing?" she asked somewhat mischievously, wanting to provoke him enough to get a response.

"We're doing it, ain't we?" He speared the remains of a cellophane wrapper with his stick and transferred it to the bag.

"Yes, but do you think it should be our responsibility?"

"World's gotten to be one big garbage dump," he said vehemently. "If you and I don't care, who will?"

Louise soon realized that she'd opened a floodgate. Harvey had made himself an expert on waste products and ways to handle them. He had strong words about local landfills, which could pollute groundwater. At best, the local one would soon be full, and new sites were hard to find. No one wanted a dump in his neighborhood.

Since he'd been forced to take his wife to a nursing home in Potterston for her dementia, he spent much of his time studying trash and recycling in all its forms. He even had a Web site where he kept in contact with like-minded people.

"The average American generates over four and a half pounds of trash every day," he said. "That's 230 million tons of trash every year."

"Surely some is recycled," Louise said.

"Less than a quarter of the total. We could recycle seventy percent if every community in the country got behind it."

"I'm trying to imagine throwing out over four pounds a day," Louise said thoughtfully.

"Here's one of the main reasons." He held up the remains of a cardboard box that had once held a basketball. "Packaging. Why do you need a heavy box to sell a kid's ball? He probably opened it in the car and threw this out the window."

Unlike Dorothy's rapid-fire chatter, Harvey's monologue on the earth's problems kept her mind occupied. The work seemed to go much faster than it had the last time, which was a very good thing. The wind had picked up, and dark clouds were massing above them.

"It looks like we're in for rain," she said after Harvey took a breather from telling her about the inadequacies of the county's recycling plan.

"Maybe."

Weather, it seemed, wasn't his major concern. He'd discovered a cache of aluminum cans at the edge of a grove of trees and was roundly condemning the people who'd left them there.

"Darn kids. Never give a thought to what the world will be like when they're my age."

Louise wasn't at all sure that kids were the culprits. Certainly the young weren't the only ones who were careless with the earth's resources. She decided against debating it though. Harvey was like a doll she'd had as a child, silent until you pulled a string to make it talk. She mused about how complicated people were. Here was a silent, some might say grouchy, man who rarely communicated with members of the congregation. But when she discovered something he was passionate about, he was eager to share his knowledge. It gave her an idea.

"You know, Harvey, the library sponsors a series of 'Know Your Community' programs. You would be the perfect person to give a presentation about what you've learned."

"I'm not much of a talker." He stopped working and looked at her with surprise.

"You don't have to be a professional speaker to participate. Just talk from your heart, and people will respond. You've taught me a lot today."

He mumbled something she didn't catch and tied off the bag they'd just finished.

"Would you like me to speak to someone at the library?"

"If you want to." He sounded noncommittal, but Louise suspected that he was considering it as a way to spread his ideas.

"I'll do it then."

Louise looked up in surprise as a drop of rain landed on her glasses. She had a tissue in her pocket to dry them, but it wouldn't be long before the rain began in earnest.

"Make yourself a raincoat," Harvey said, taking one of their large trash bags and punching holes for his head and arms. "But when you throw it away, be sure to tie it in knots. Birds can get tangled in loose sheets of plastic and die. That's no way to treat our feathered friends."

She would have preferred to quit then, but they were so close to finishing that no one was making any move to leave.

Harvey picked up the pace, forcing Louise to hustle to keep up. It was her turn to hold the bags, and the one filled with cans was nearly full. She shook it down, hoping she could finish without needing to begin a new one.

A few more drops fell on her arms, but the way the wind was pushing the clouds, there was no predicting when or if a deluge would begin.

She was vaguely aware of several cars that passed on their side of the road, then a faded blue pickup went by with a sudden burst of noise.

The heavy wind had loosened a tarp covering the bed, and the driver was losing the load. The truck veered to the side and came to a stop, and a dark-haired woman in jeans raced to the back. She tried to secure the tarp, but it was like a sail in the wind, flapping so hard that she found it impossible to get a grasp.

Jack wasn't far away, and he sprinted toward her. He was too late. The truck had been packed with empty aluminum cans, and the wind took many of them. They clattered down the road and rolled in all directions, some even becoming airborne.

Louise and Harvey hurried over to the pickup, as did other crew members who noticed what was happening, but it was soon clear that much of the woman's load was lost. Several men managed to secure the tarp, but the barrage of empty cans had scattered in all directions.

"I can't believe this." The thin-faced woman seemed near tears. "My children hunted cans all winter. All our neighbors saved them. I was on my way to the recycling plant to turn them in. The kids were going to add the money to what they've already saved to buy a calf. What am I going to tell them? It's all my fault."

"It's not your fault that the wind is so strong," Jack said in a comforting voice.

"No, but I tried to save money by not putting them in

plastic trash bags. They're not cheap, you know. Now my boys won't be able to get their calf."

"Sure they will." Harvey took off his cap to save it from the wind, and the fine white fluff on his head was standing upright. "We got plenty of people to pick them up. Can't have cans spoiling our nice clean roadway."

"You mean pick them all up?" The woman looked incredulous.

Jack shrugged his approval, and no one voiced any protest.

Louise looked at the shiny dots that were still being carried far afield by the wind and had her doubts. Then she looked at the careworn face of the woman and knew they had to try.

"I'm Louise," she said, stepping forward and nodding at the others. "This is Jack, and this is Harvey. We're members of Grace Chapel, doing our mile of highway cleanup. We're practically pros at trash cleanup."

"I'm Beth."

She held out her hand, and Louise was surprised by how cold it felt. More raindrops splashed on her outstretched arm, and several other church members made makeshift raincoats for themselves. Harvey offered one to Beth, but she had a rain slicker in the cab of the pickup.

Louise chased cans, grabbing them on the fly and finding them lodged among the greenery on the roadside. She was tempted to ask, "Why me, Lord?" Instead she laughed aloud and decided to make a bizarre game of it. She gave every can she picked up a name, entertaining herself by thinking of odd and unusual ones.

"Ah, here you are, Herkimer," she said tossing a soda can into her bag. "I have you, Bleecker, you too, Artesia."

The rain was playing games too, teasing them with mild sprinkles, then dumping a cloudload on the scurrying can-hunters. Louise's sleeves were soaked and the rain in her hair was dripping down her face.

Jack drove his borrowed truck ahead to harvest the ones that had gone the farthest, and passing cars slowed to see what was going on. One man even parked and joined them, filling a bag and leaving it beside the road before he drove away without telling anyone who he was.

"There you are, Pickett," said Louise, spotting a ginger ale can that had lodged in a bush. She made her way down a rather steep incline to retrieve it, glad that the noise of the wind and rain drowned out her rather eccentric conversation with the can.

One minute she was cautiously making her way toward the container, and the next she was sitting on the slippery, grass-covered slope. She stood up gingerly and decided that nothing was hurt but her pride. Was this what had happened to Jane, upright one moment and down the next before her brain could even register the fall? It would explain why Jane had seemed so puzzled immediately after she got home.

She picked up Pickett but decided to stop naming the cans. She needed to concentrate on staying upright.

Rain was making visibility a problem, and all the workers gradually gathered by the pickup. Harvey hoisted himself up onto the bed, leaving just enough tarp unsecured to shove everyone's bags into the space under it.

Jack returned with the big truck and donated all the cans they'd gathered that day toward purchasing a calf for Beth's sons. There were so many that some bags had to go on the seat beside her. Louise thought Beth was crying when she drove away, but it was hard to tell in the rain.

Louise's hair was plastered to her skull, the overalls were soaked wherever they hadn't been covered by the makeshift raincape and her shoes squished when she walked. Harvey drove her to the inn, and she went around to the back door, hoping to get to her room without alarming her sisters.

She was taking off her shoes and socks when Alice found her.

Alice was speechless. Louise was soaked to the bone, but she was grinning broadly as she used a clean towel in the storage room to blot herself dry enough to go upstairs without leaving a trail.

"I know. I look like something the cat dragged in," she said with a laugh.

"Why didn't you stop working when it started to rain?"

Alice listened to an abbreviated version of the big can chase. Her sister was badly in need of a hot shower and dry clothes, so Alice didn't ask her any more questions. Louise seemed jubilant about her work that day, so no doubt she would have more to say when she'd had a chance to recover.

"Would you mind if I take a short nap?" Louise asked as she started toward her room. "I have two lessons after school is out, but I really need to recharge my battery."

"Of course, I don't mind. Jane may have had the same idea. She went up to her room, and I haven't seen her for hours. I'll stay down here and watch for our new guests. All three empty rooms are booked for tonight."

Left alone, Alice made a mental list of all the jobs that needed to be done. She opted to dust the parlor first, not that Louise's students were likely to notice, but because it was way past time to do it. Before she could begin, the phone rang.

"Grace Chapel Inn. This is Alice."

"Alice, I'm glad I caught you at home."

"Mark, how are you?"

Unlike many older men, Mark Graves still had the resonant voice of a younger person. She had instantly recognized it, and it still had the power to warm her heart. She couldn't think of a nicer surprise than a call from him on this gloomy, rainy day.

"Great. I'm going to a conference in New Jersey tomorrow and Wednesday. On Thursday there's a Phillies game in town. I wonder if there's any chance you could join me there.

I have tickets, and there's a new show at the I-Max theater that you might enjoy too. It's been too long since I saw you."

"That sounds wonderful, but . . ."

"But?"

"We're in a bit of a bind at the inn. Jane had a fall and has to keep off her feet for at least another two weeks. We've been scrambling to cover for her."

"Don't tell me you've become the chef?" he teased.

Mark was a good cook himself, and there was nothing he loved more than firing up an outside grill. Alice could imagine him, her distinguished friend with his handsome features and graying temples, in an apron with silly sayings on it.

"No, we have a substitute cook to make breakfast, but Louise and I have learned how much Jane really does to keep the inn running. Covering for her has us stretched thin. It wouldn't be fair to Louise if I left, not to mention that I've been putting in quite a few hours at the hospital. I'm really sorry, Mark. I'd love to see you."

"Don't worry. Summer is just beginning. I'm sure we'll be able to get together soon. We're expecting a new Siberian tiger at the zoo. Once she's settled into her new environment, I'll be able to get away more easily. I hope you'll give me a rain check."

"Of course."

They talked for nearly half an hour. Alice sometimes marveled at how much they found to say to each other, even though their career experiences were far apart. Usually she felt buoyed up and happy after a conversation with Mark, but today was different. She hung up with a heavy heart.

Maybe it was because she regretted her decision not to join him for a baseball game. Neither Jane nor Louise would have wanted her to turn down an opportunity to spend time with Mark. Somehow they could manage without her. The hospital could run without her. Had she just put another brick on the wall that kept them apart?

She thought about the new Siberian tiger, the rare white beast that Mark especially loved. He was so enthusiastic about its arrival that the phone line had fairly crackled with excitement when he spoke of it. She was happy for his success even though she was intimidated by the raw power of some of the savage animals with which Mark dealt. If she'd followed him all those years ago, would she ever have learned to love wildlife the way he did? She didn't think so. The tiger would frighten her even if Mark's zoo had unbreakable plate glass separating it from spectators.

Wendell sidled up to her in an affectionate mood. She scooped him up and held him, stroking his head until he purred like a kitten. Her gray and black striped tabby was quite enough cat for her. She set him down on his white-tipped paws and led the way to the kitchen to give him a treat. She didn't even want to think about the great slabs of raw meat that Mark would give to his Siberian.

Emily Cleary's difficult decision, whether or not to leave her career and marry Henry Toyer, had made Alice think more than usual about her relationship with Mark. But in a moment of stunning clarity, she realized that they were in an entirely different situation. They had a deep and abiding friendship and respected each other's responsibilities. Mark wouldn't want her to let her sisters down any more than she would want him to miss the thrill of adding a rare and exotic animal to the zoo's collection. Love was a complicated emotion, but part of it was the freedom to be yourself.

Chapter Fourteen

Louise was so late for breakfast Tuesday morning that she expected to fend for herself. Instead Salty was still in the kitchen, occupying himself by cleaning the cupboard doors.

"Here's the sleepy head," he said in a jovial tone. "You've missed my French toast with orange butter."

"That's all right. I'll get myself some cereal."

"Not while I'm on duty. I have a petite soufflé au fromage ready to go in the oven. I made it with Gruyère cheese. I seem to remember that you especially like it."

"You made a soufflé just for me? You didn't need to do that."

"My pleasure. The oven is hot, so you'll have it in twelve to fifteen minutes. I just finished baking a pan of chocolate meringue cookies, a little treat for your lunch. Meanwhile, I'll make some toast points with cinnamon sugar on that honey-wheat you like. You can have your grapefruit while you wait."

He put pink grapefruit with the sections neatly cut and garnished with a red cherry in front of her. Her instinct was to protest. It really wasn't necessary for him to go to so much trouble, but she knew by now that there was no stopping Salty when his mind was made up.

The soufflé, baked in a small white ceramic dish, was

light, fluffy and perfectly browned. Louise felt like royalty as she ate the breakfast especially prepared for her.

Salty didn't hover while she ate, but she knew he was waiting for his session on the piano. She was less than enthusiastic, but how could she begrudge Salty his lesson when he went to so much trouble fixing a special breakfast for her?

"I'll be with you in a minute," he said after she had finished and thanked him. "I'm running low on dish towels, so I'll start a load in the washing machine."

He seemed to be taking on new duties every day, but there was no denying that he was helpful. Louise was most grateful for his enthusiastic contributions to the inn.

She went to the parlor and sorted through his sheet music while she waited for him to join her. He always left the kitchen immaculate, and she tried to wait patiently.

He'd made good progress on his grandfather's song, especially after she insisted that he not sing during the lesson. Fortunately the tune was a simple one, and his willingness to practice was impressive. If only she could inspire little Nina to put half that much effort into her lessons.

Louise had been too busy to give much thought to the problem of her reluctant student, but she really did have to find a way to encourage her. Either that, or tell her mother that the lessons were a waste of time. She was reluctant to do so, but sooner or later the parent would expect to hear some progress.

"Ready or not, here I am," Salty said, coming into the parlor and taking his place on the piano bench.

"How many pieces do you want to play for your veterans' group?" Louise asked, thinking that they should concentrate on just a few.

"My grandfather's, of course, then maybe two others that are more familiar. I'm leaning toward 'Over There' and 'It's a Long Way to Tipperary.' There's something I have to tell you, though. I haven't been honest with you."

"Oh?"

"I didn't quit piano lessons just because of sports. The truth is . . ." He shrugged and sounded reluctant to go on.

"Why did you quit?" she encouraged him.

"The recitals did me in. I could play a piece just fine at home, but when I had to perform in front of people, I fell apart. I'm not a shy guy by nature, but doing my stuff in front of an audience made my blood run cold. I'm a lot older now, and I hope I've gotten over it, but I want to know the World War I songs so well that I can't possibly freeze."

"I've had students like that," Louise said thoughtfully. "Stage fright is hard to overcome. Fortunately you'll be playing for friends, not music critics or judges. I think you'll do just fine."

"Yeah, but the guys take talent night seriously. If I make a mess of the songs, my friends will never let me hear the end of it."

"Do you still want to try?"

"Yes, it's important for me to do it as a tribute to my grandfather, father and brother. They faced bullets. I should be able to handle musical notes. I've never thought I lived up to the family tradition, being a cook and all."

"What's that saying, 'An army travels on its stomach'? I'm sure that must be true of the navy too. You were doing something absolutely essential, and you should be proud of it."

"Well, maybe, but I'm still worried that I'll lose my nerve when I sit down to play."

"Maybe what you need is a recital of your own, a chance to practice in front of people before the big night," Louise said pensively. "Let me think about it."

Salty's lesson went very well, which only affirmed Louise's belief that anyone can improve if he or she is willing to practice, practice, practice. She left him in the parlor, closing the door on her way out. She admired his determination, but if she heard "He's a Doughboy from Ohio" one more time, she might decide it was better to fix the guests' breakfasts herself.

She had a long list of chores to do before it was time for her regular lessons, but she couldn't get Nina out of her mind. Louise was blessed with some outstanding students, but working with the talented ones was much easier and more pleasurable than struggling with an unwilling child. There had to be a way to ignite her interest, but so far it had evaded Louise. None of the techniques that she used with beginners was at all successful with Nina.

For now, there were chores to do. It was recycling day, and if she didn't carry out their bins right away, they might miss the truck when it came. After everything her trash-picking partner had told her yesterday, their collection of cans, bottles and newspapers didn't seem so insignificant. That reminded her she needed to call the town library. She was pretty sure they would welcome a program on solid waste management, and Harvey Racklin had convinced her that he had the knowledge to provide it.

Fortunately the recyclers came every week, so the inn's containers weren't overflowing. When she thought about it, she realized that the inn did generate a lot of waste. Multiply what they put out by many millions, and a virtual mountain of trash had to be handled in the United States every year. Maybe when her aunt got home, she could talk to her friend, Lloyd Tynan, Acorn Hill's mayor. The town could recycle a lot more, especially paper products, according to Harvey.

Louise carried out the blue tub of newspapers first. The town's only paper, the *Acorn Nutshell*, was a weekly, so there wasn't much to recycle from that, but Alice liked to pick up a Philadelphia paper from time to time. Louise bought a national paper several times a week from the vending machine in front of the General Store. The guests also left behind newspapers, so they had a significant amount of newsprint to recycle.

To save time on the second trip, Louise piled the tub of cans on top of the one holding glass and carried the stack to the street. When she bent to put them down, the top one tipped over, spilling out the contents.

The wind was still brisk today, and, predictably, the cans started rolling down the street toward the chapel.

Louise groaned and gave chase. This couldn't be happening again.

She caught some close to home, but others seemed to have a life of their own and merrily clattered down the street, moving faster than she could. When she did catch them, she could only carry so many at a time. She had to hurry back to the tub every time her hands were full. It was a small task compared to gathering the pickup load yesterday, but she was annoyed by her own carelessness.

After several trips back to the tub, she made a quick count, wondering if she had them all. But no, she distinctly remembered an orange soda can left by a guest. It wasn't a brand that was sold locally, and the shiny container should have been easy to spot.

She struggled briefly with her conscience but decided she couldn't leave it to clutter up the neighborhood. She walked down the left-hand side of the street, then crossed to check the bushes on the other side, sure that it couldn't have gone much farther. At last she spotted an orange glint in the shallow drainage ditch beside the road.

"There you are, Jasper," she said, climbing down to fetch it.

She walked back to the inn laughing at herself. She'd done it again—named a can. Maybe it was because it had taunted her with its great escape, just as the cans from the pickup had yesterday.

She tossed the container into the bin, then stared at it thoughtfully. The errant soda can had just given her an idea.

∞

Jane wasn't sure why she wanted to work in her room instead of the office. She could shut the door in either room, and what she was doing wasn't that secret. Of course, she really didn't want Salty to see her work at this stage. It was possible he might seek her out in the office, but it wasn't likely. He'd taken over her kitchen as if he'd been born to cook breakfast at the inn, but when he was through there for the morning, he usually went right to the parlor for his lesson and a practice session.

She'd spread out the series of pen-and-ink sketches, each one done from memory. She could probably do better, of course, if she sketched Salty as he worked, but that would spoil the surprise. She intended to put the best ones in a folder as a going-away gift for his helping them so much.

Adding a touch of color, scarlet red, emerald green or bright yellow, to each one had helped them come alive. Although she had drawn them as caricatures, she didn't want Salty to come off as silly. They were intended to compliment his culinary talents and thank him for all he'd done.

She was fairly well satisfied with two of them, but she wanted at least three good ones, if not more. She rejected one because she'd exaggerated his girth and another because the nose wasn't quite right. What she wanted to do this morning was make a pencil sketch showing him in the grocery store. It was her way of saying she forgave him for making her ride that rolling disaster-mobile.

Should she draw him squeezing lettuce or pinching grapefruit? No, that was too ordinary. She needed to give the grocery scene a little more thought.

Louise was excited. What she needed was a list of silly names, ones that a child would recognize and find amusing. There was nothing in the inn that filled the bill, but she knew an expert, her friend Viola Reed, who owned Nine Lives Bookstore. Her shop was only a short walk away.

Alice was working at the hospital, a last-minute assignment because a pediatric nurse had called in sick. Jane was . . . well, she didn't know exactly where Jane was, maybe in her room.

She looked at the reservations list and saw that no new guests should arrive before late afternoon. If she hurried, she wouldn't be missed. This was something that had to be done before her first lesson of the day.

Just then the phone rang.

"Grace Chapel Inn. This is Louise."

"Harvey Racklin here."

"Oh, Harvey, I haven't had a chance to call about speaking at the library, but I'll take care of it today for sure."

"Changed my mind."

"About speaking?"

"I'm no speech-giver."

"Oh, I don't think they expect anything very formal. Just tell people something of what you've learned about solid waste management. There must be more recycling that we can do right here in Acorn Hill. I can't get the four and a half pounds of garbage per person out of my mind."

"I can't do it."

"I'm sure they could work out a time that fits your schedule."

"Got nothing to do with schedules. I thought it over, and I'm not going to do it."

"Well, if you really feel that way."

"I do."

"I'm sorry to hear that." She was curious about his change of heart but didn't know whether she should ask why. He could have a very personal reason for declining.

"Talking's not my thing." He sounded angry about it, but then, Harvey could be easily riled.

"I'm sure you would do a fine job. The things you told me yesterday were really interesting."

"If you want to know, I can't speak in front of people. I get the cold shakes. My stomach cramps up. I forget what I wanted to say."

"Oh, that's too bad."

Harvey Racklin, a man who never seemed to care what

others thought of him, suffered from stage fright just as Salty did. It wasn't a rational matter, so she didn't think she could reason away his anxiety. Still, he was such a fount of good information about recycling that it would be a shame if he didn't tell others what he knew.

"Let me think about it," she said. "Maybe there's a painless way to share all your good information."

"I'm not making a speech."

"I understand. Well, thank you for letting me know. I'll talk to you soon."

She ran possibilities through her mind as she walked to Viola's bookstore. Maybe the local newspaper could interview him. Or he could make a videotape that could be shown to civic groups. She could imagine his objections to both, but it still seemed a shame if he didn't bring his recycling message to others.

This was Jane's kind of problem, a cause that was sure to interest her when she was back on her feet. Louise didn't know where to go with it at the moment.

She only hoped that Viola had time to help her with the more immediate problem of Nina. Although she'd never had children herself, the bookstore owner put great emphasis on literature for young people. She might know how to trigger interest in a reluctant student.

The inn was too quiet. Jane could hear the whistle of the wind in the trees and the familiar creak of the steps as she made her way downstairs, but otherwise silence reigned in the big old house.

Apparently Salty had abandoned his practice session early, since the parlor was empty. The guests had checked out, except for Emily Cleary, and Jane hadn't seen her yet today. Alice was working at the hospital, of course, but where was Louise? It was unlike her to leave the inn without saying anything.

On an ordinary day, Jane wouldn't have given a thought to her sister's whereabouts. That she did so today only emphasized how tedious it was not to be able to go about her usual routine.

Crutches weren't as limiting as they'd first seemed, and she was getting proficient at balancing on one leg. As her bad leg got weaker, her good one seemed to get stronger. Certainly there were some jobs she could do in the kitchen. She missed the everyday activities of a busy day at the inn. She especially missed the sheer pleasure of creating luscious meals, both for the guests and her sisters. Her fingers itched to measure, stir and concoct.

The kitchen disappointed her. She checked it out from sink to stove, from fridge to floor, and found absolutely nothing that needed doing. The cupboard doors were spotless, the stove top glistened and the shelves in the fridge were arranged with military precision. A casserole dish was ready to pop in the oven for their dinner. Salty hadn't left a single thing for her to straighten, scrub or rearrange.

She sat at the table and stared bleakly at her perfectly ordered kitchen. The man was a wonder, his cooking was fantastic, and she desperately wanted him to leave. She wasn't proud of her attitude, but she felt utterly useless. She'd been replaced by a cook who seemed to be at least her equal, and the tedium of not working at her specialty bothered her more than the pain in her leg.

After what she regarded to be a good sulk, she slowly made her way out of the kitchen. When all was said and done, there was still desk work to do, credit card slips to process, entries to make in the books. She would rather eat fried worms than do the accounting, in spite of all that Bert Frame had taught her. But fair was fair, and she'd undertaken this job of Louise's.

❧

Louise was sure of one thing as the time for Nina's lesson approached. Viola's idea was too complicated. She'd made a list of favorite children's characters, but they wouldn't mean a thing unless the eight-year-old was familiar with all of them. It seemed unlikely.

She still liked her idea of naming the notes. Playing a game with the soda cans had helped her get through a tedious chore, but whatever she did with Nina had to be simple.

Salty liked the piano best when he could belt out the lyrics as he played. Louise's mind was still playing with possibilities when Nina came to the parlor door to begin her lesson.

She was a sweet girl, her flaxen hair hanging in long pigtails and her face made more earnest by little round wire glasses.

"Nina, come in. Did you have a good day at school?"

Bad start, Louise immediately thought. It was the question adults always asked, and she didn't want their lesson to be colored by any setbacks her pupil might have had in the classroom.

"Fine."

"Shall we get started?" She decided not to ask whether Nina had practiced. She didn't want to give the girl a reason to fib when it would soon be obvious whether or not she had.

Louise resisted an urge to cover her ears as the child stumbled through the scales she'd supposedly been practicing. She wanted to release Nina from the drudgery of learning something she was strongly resisting, but that would mean admitting defeat, not something Louise was comfortable doing.

"Let's try those scales another way," Louise said, deciding to go with her silly idea as a last resort. "Pretend that the notes are animals, and every time you hit the right one, I'll make a noise for that animal."

Nina stared at her with round blue eyes but didn't protest.

"D is for dog," Louise said.

Nina hit the right key, and Louise gave a ferocious bark.

"Now what would be good for E?"

"Elephant," her student immediately said.

Louise wasn't at all sure she could trumpet like an elephant, but she gave it a try and was rewarded by a burst of laughter.

"Now F."

"Frog."

"Ribbet, ribbet."

Louise didn't hold back. She gave a loud baa that she hoped was like a goat, did her best to gibber like an ape, and cheeped like a bird. The cat's meow was easy, and they ended the scale with another D for duck.

"Quack, quack," Louise said, laughing along with Nina when they'd finished. "Now try it again, and you make the animal noises."

Nina picked out the notes, D E F# G A B C# D, making the appropriate sounds. When she finished, she giggled with pleasure.

On impulse, Louise decided to go back to the very first tune she'd tried to teach her, "Mary Had a Little Lamb." Even that simplest of songs hadn't gone well, but she thought of a way to infuse some life into it.

"I've already done that one," Nina complained.

"Yes, but you only played it. This time try playing and singing the words."

After a couple of false starts, Nina did exactly that. Amazingly, she played much better when she sang along. Apparently she really enjoyed singing, and with good reason. She had a sweet, clear voice, and she picked up the tune almost effortlessly. When she'd mastered some of the basics on the piano, she might be a good candidate for voice lessons. This gave Louise something positive to discuss with her mother.

Who would guess that chasing cans along a highway could lead to a better lesson for a reluctant pupil? Louise smiled, remembering that God works in mysterious ways.

Jane pushed aside the account book, surprised at how quickly she'd done the little bit that needed doing. Bert Frame's advice had helped her breeze through the few simple things that were needed to keep current. In fact, if she did it every day as Louise did, the job was no harder than setting the table or loading the dishwasher. They had a good system, thanks to her sister.

This didn't mean that she wouldn't be immensely grateful when she could get back to her own job, but she did vow not to procrastinate as she had last week.

She was on the cot, leg propped up according to doctor's instructions, reading one of her gourmet cooking magazines when Louise popped into the study.

"How did your lesson go?"

"If you can imagine me quacking like a duck and trying to sound like an elephant, it went very well indeed."

She smiled and left the room, leaving Jane mystified.

Chapter Fifteen

"These curried eggs are really delicious," Alice said, savoring a bite of toast topped with another Salty special. "I've never heard of adding peanuts, but it gives them an interesting crunch."

"The secret is in the herbs," he said, joining them at the kitchen table Tuesday morning to eat his own breakfast.

"Whenever I see creamed eggs," Louise said, "I remember my homemaking teacher in eighth grade. She was a fanatic about making good cream sauce. By the end of the school year, I hoped never to see it again. But I have to agree, this is really tasty."

"Yes, it's good," Jane said, although she didn't seem to be eating much.

Alice reminded herself that she absolutely had to work in the garden today. Things were growing like crazy after the spring rains, and at the moment the Howard sisters were specializing in weeds.

There was something else on her mind.

"I keep thinking about the lovely time I had with Emily and Henry," she said. "I do wish there was something I could do to thank them. They were so nice to me at the art show."

"Make them a dinner here at the inn," Salty said.

"I think they rather value the time they can spend alone," Alice said. "They have a big decision to make."

"All the more reason to give them a romantic dinner for two at Grace Chapel Inn," Salty said.

"You know, that's not a bad idea." Alice pursed her lips thoughtfully, considering the options.

"There's no reason why I can't help you put together something nice. With you to do the legwork, I can make it really special," Jane said.

"Count me in," Salty said. "I'm free Thursday and Friday. In fact, I think Hope would like a little time to herself. Having her old uncle around twenty-four/seven can't be easy."

"I can invite them and see if they're interested," Alice said, looking at Jane for confirmation.

"Do," she said. "If they agree, we can work out the details."

Alice volunteered to clean the kitchen after breakfast, but Salty wouldn't hear of it. As a result, she was left with free time to work in the garden, and she hastened to get at it. She could practically hear the weeds growing, taking over every bed before she'd even planted flowers in some of them.

The day was starting out warm. May was nearly over, and by noon it would be downright hot. Alice assembled the implements in a small wheelbarrow and decided to work first in the area closest to the street. There were several flats of impatiens to be planted, and that seemed a good place for them. No doubt Jane would have other ideas when she was able to do the work herself, but lately she hadn't shown much interest in the garden.

Jane's indifference to the garden was a cause for concern, since she hadn't even sketched a rough plan for Alice to follow. She needed a project to stimulate her enthusiasm, and a dinner for Emily and Henry might be just the thing. Of course, Salty had volunteered, and Alice couldn't turn him down after all he'd done for them. Would Jane enjoy working on a dinner with him? She did have experience in a large restaurant kitchen with several chefs working at the same time.

First, of course, she had to invite Emily and Henry. The opportunity came sooner than she expected when Emily saw her working and came over to chat.

"Good morning, Alice. You have quite a garden here."

"Good morning, Emily. I'm afraid it's gotten away from us this spring. Jane usually cares for it. She's the one with a green thumb."

"I thought I would visit the bookstore this morning. I need something to read on the plane going home."

"Before you do, there's something I want to ask you." Alice straightened and put aside her hoe. "We'd like to fix a nice dinner for you and Henry here at the inn."

"How sweet of you, but I couldn't put you to all that trouble."

"Jane would be thrilled to plan it, and both Salty and I will help her. I don't mean a family meal, though, just dinner for the two of you."

"I'm going home Saturday, you know."

"Salty suggested Thursday or Friday."

"All right, I'd love to, and I'm sure Henry will agree. Friday would work best. We're having dinner with some of his family members Thursday. Just let me know what time."

"Would seven be all right?"

"Lovely. We'll both look forward to it. And we're not fussy eaters. Fix whatever is easy for you."

Alice didn't say anything, but an easy dinner wasn't at all what they had in mind.

Now that Jane had a special objective, she tackled her cookbook collection with gusto, marking page after page with sticky notes. Alice and Salty could help her, but she was going to plan the meal, an extraordinary one that would showcase her talent. Not only had she grown fond of Emily, one of the sweetest guests they'd had in a long time, but she was itching to work her magic once again.

Maybe, she admitted to herself, she was a bit too eager to show Salty what she could do. Was it wrong to be competitive? Chefs tended to compete ferociously to produce the tastiest dishes and best presentations, but she didn't want dinner to become a contest with their substitute cook. She was only too aware of how much he'd helped them, asking little in return. Although she would have liked to do the meal alone, she knew his feelings would be hurt if she refused to include him in the preparation.

By Wednesday morning, she was ready for their after-breakfast meeting to plan the menu. As soon as all the guests left the dining room, Alice, Jane and Salty gathered at the kitchen table for a conference, Louise having excused herself from all things culinary on the grounds that the others didn't need her.

"The fanciest meal I ever had was in Rome," Salty began. "A friend and I were in the restaurant four or five hours. When we sat down, they brought a basket of bread and another of hard, spicy sausages arranged like some kind of weird leafless plant. Our waiter kept bringing different courses without asking what we wanted. I thought it must be family style, everyone getting the same things. Just when I decided we'd had a full meal, it was time to order the main entrée. What really impressed me was that the waiter knew every ingredient in every dish. He described them so well it was almost impossible to make a choice. I think a Roman style dinner would be the ticket. Nothing smells, tastes or looks better than authentic Italian."

"You may be right," Jane conceded, "but I don't think Emily would be up for such a heavy meal. I had in mind something light but elegant, Rock Cornish hens with wild rice stuffing. I like them served with garlic roasted spring vegetables and homemade hard rolls."

Salty rested his chin on his fist, reminding Jane of a bulldog who's just had his dinner dish pulled away. She considered sketching him that way but decided it wouldn't be flattering.

"My spaghetti with clams is world-class," he said. "I use butter and extra virgin olive oil, but the real secret is fresh herbs. We could serve it as the pasta course, then go on to the hens."

"Alice?" Jane looked at her sister for support.

"I'll leave it up to you experts."

Jane sighed and leaned back on the chair. "Tell you what, let me do the main course with Rock Cornish hens, and you can choose the appetizer and dessert."

"Sounds fair," he agreed. "Do you have a chafing dish? I haven't run across one yet."

"It's stored in the buffet in the dining room."

"My hot clam dip wowed 'em at the officers' club. I called it . . ."

"The Salty special," Jane and Alice said in unison.

He bellowed with laughter, and Jane decided their collaboration would work.

Jane wanted to hug her sister when she agreed to do the grocery shopping with Salty on Friday morning. Jane could call ahead and reserve the Cornish hens she needed. She would brief Alice on exactly what ingredients to buy, and there was no reason why everything shouldn't go smoothly, no reason at all.

When Friday afternoon came, Jane was eager to get to work. She'd chosen hard rolls to prepare first because they required quite a bit of attention. They took longer to rise because there was no sugar in the dough, and she looked forward to feeling the dough under her fingers when she formed it into golf-ball size pieces.

The secret to perfect hard rolls was to create steam to form the crunchy outer layer. Jane favored putting ice cubes in the bottom of the oven, although some bakers used a pan of boiling water. She liked to brush the rolls with a mixture of cold water and egg white and sprinkle on sesame seeds.

Salty had mentioned hot clam dip as his appetizer, but he was secretive about dessert. Still, it became obvious that he was making a chocolate mousse when they both began working in the kitchen Friday afternoon.

Jane suspected that his appetizers would involve more than the clam dip, but they had an unspoken agreement not to get involved in the other's work. She was enjoying herself so much that it hardly bothered her to stand on one leg. When she first started, Alice hovered nearby, eager to fetch and carry, but Jane convinced her to set the table instead.

Jane couldn't fault Salty for being less than forthcoming. She took pains to conceal the seasonings she added to the wild rice stuffing, not to mention the ingredients for a subtle lemon-based glaze she painted on the hens. No chef worth his or her salt would give away all the little extras that led to a unique, perfect creation.

"Hello, is anyone here? Jane! Where are you?"

A familiar voice rang through the foyer, and Jane grabbed her crutches to go greet the unexpected visitor. She wasn't fast enough. Florence strode into the kitchen before Jane could get underway.

"I've been so neglectful since you've been laid up," Florence said. "I wanted to make up for it by bringing you a tomato aspic. It's a specialty of mine. I put in lots of fresh, crunchy vegetables and top it with a homemade dressing."

She put a covered pan on the table and looked around at the controlled chaos in the kitchen.

"Have I interrupted something? Oh dear, Jane, don't tell me you're cooking. I understood that you were to rest your leg for three weeks."

"Rest but not rust," Jane said. "Florence Simpson, this is Saul Loughry, our substitute cook."

"Everyone calls me Salty," he said, nodding but not offering his flour-coated hand.

Jane had his number now. He was making cheese straws, a nice enough appetizer but not necessary when he was already planning to serve the hot clam dip. Was this his own version of a Roman feast? Did he want their guests to be too full to enjoy her main course?

Oh no, there was that competitive urge again. Jane made a conscious effort to get beyond it and give Florence her attention.

"Thank you for the aspic. How is your toe? I still feel bad about landing on your foot."

"It's fine now, thank you. It looks like you're cooking for a banquet—or a party." Florence's voice had the slightly hurt tone of someone who hadn't been invited.

"No, only a dinner for one of our guests and her friend, a thank-you occasion."

"If there's anything I can do—" Florence began.

"Glad you asked, Flo," Salty quickly said. "I need someone to shave bitter chocolate for me. Wash your hands, and I'll find you something to use as an apron. Wouldn't want to get your pretty pink dress dirty."

Florence opened her mouth, but no words came out. Salty had just accomplished the impossible: He left Florence speechless.

Before she could protest, he found an oversized dish towel and tied it around her neck like a bib.

"I only dropped in—" Florence sputtered.

"What I need are the finest possible shavings from this chunk of bitter chocolate. You look like a handy person with a knife, but would you rather use a carrot scraper? That works pretty well if you're not comfortable with a really sharp blade."

"I'm very good with a knife," Florence said primly, "but—"

"Wonderful. I won't need a lot, just enough to garnish the whipped topping on the chocolate mousse. I made a little extra just for sampling. You wouldn't like to taste a Salty-special mousse, would you, Flo?"

"I don't know—"

"Here, you can work at the end of the table where you won't be in the way."

Jane had never seen a docile Florence. She sat and scraped chocolate, her face puckered in concentration. Salty loped over and checked on her from time to time.

"This bit is a little thick. There's a knack to it, so keep practicing," he encouraged her.

Jane didn't know whether to rescue Florence from the chore or let her do Salty's bidding. Florence was the least likely person in Acorn Hill to need help in declining a job that she didn't want to do, but she looked utterly confused. Still, she diligently worked at shaving the dark chunk of chocolate as though she were a raw recruit on one of Salty's ships.

"Now you have the knack," he proclaimed as he cut his cheese straws into strips on the floured board. "Good girl. You've earned a taste of a Salty special."

He stopped what he was doing, went to the fridge and spooned out a small portion of the mousse, dropping on a bit of whipped cream and a smidgen of shaved chocolate.

"Just a bite," he said. "Don't want you to spoil your supper."

He dipped a spoon into the sample and held it in front of Florence's mouth.

Jane's jaw dropped. She expected Florence to protest against being fed, but she savored the spoonful, then smiled broadly, praising his chocolate treat with every adjective possible.

"Simply luscious. You must give me your recipe. It's beyond words, absolutely fabulous. I don't know when I've tasted anything so good."

Salty beamed. "I suppose I could be naughty and give you just a bit more."

"Oh no," Florence protested weakly.

He let her consume the second helping on her own, but the smile didn't leave either of their faces. Jane was frankly curious, but she wouldn't let herself ask for a taste. When Salty offered, she politely declined.

"I have too much to do. Timing is everything when you're serving a gourmet meal," she said by way of explanation.

Salty knew that, of course, but he was polite enough not to say so.

Before she left, Florence scrubbed pans, wiped off the counters and sampled a chip with Salty's hot clam dip, literally smacking her lips in appreciation. She didn't seem to notice the wet dishwater spot on the front of her spring frock.

Alice was just a bit nervous, although she couldn't pin down any reason to be. The dinner was only a gesture of friendship, and it wouldn't in any way influence the decision that Emily and Henry had to make. Still, she couldn't shake the feeling that she was playing Cupid, providing a romantic setting for two people she liked and admired.

Henry came to join Emily for the dinner promptly at seven, and Alice directed them to the parlor where Salty had set up his savory appetizers and a bottle of mineral water in an ice bucket. He declared that it would take half an hour for them to do justice to his creations.

He and Jane had elected her as waitress, and they all agreed that she was the only one the couple would see during the course of the meal. It would make the setting much more tranquil if the three of them weren't running in and out.

When it came time to serve the main course in the dining room, Alice was proud of her sister's culinary skills. The small, golden brown birds were arranged on the inn's best china plates with garlic-roasted fresh carrot chunks, mushrooms, tiny red potatoes, zucchini and onions on the side. As always when Jane was at her best, the presentation was colorful and artful, the sign of a master chef. A linen-covered basket held the hard rolls with perfectly browned crusts, and Alice's mouth watered at the thought of biting into one.

Once the couple had been served, Louise joined the others in the kitchen, and the four of them enjoyed the same meal without using the best china. Alice had given the couple a tiny glass bell to ring if they needed anything, wanting to ensure their privacy without neglecting to serve them.

"This is absolutely wonderful," Louise said, complimenting both Jane and Salty.

They'd finished their meal, sampled the chocolate mousse set aside for them and cleaned up the kitchen before they heard the tinkle of the bell. Despite the earlier decision to have just one server, Jane insisted that Salty present the dessert since it was his masterpiece. He took off his apron and carried two stemware dessert cups into the dining room on a silver tray that had once belonged to their grandmother.

Afterward, Emily and Henry came to the kitchen to offer their profuse thanks for the lovely meal. Alice was concerned about their decision, but nothing they said gave her the slightest clue.

"We'll visit awhile on your porch if you don't mind," Henry said.

Emily sighed. "We've had perfect weather for a perfect dinner. I don't know how we can thank you enough."

Salty went home, and her sisters went up to their rooms after the kitchen was cleaned to his satisfaction, but Alice was too wide awake to settle down. She went out the back door for a stroll around the neighborhood, soothed as always by the spire of the chapel outlined against the tranquil blue of the sky. Her life was so deeply gratifying that she wanted to sing aloud in the quiet of the evening.

She silently prayed as she walked, asking God to bless her friends, Emily and Henry, and guide them in making the decision best for both of them. Without realizing it, she walked for half an hour.

The porch light was on, but that was normal in the evening. She didn't see any sign of Henry's car, so she assumed that he'd left. She was going up the front steps when she heard her name spoken softly from the darkness at the end of the porch.

"Alice."

"Oh, Emily, I didn't see you there."

"I hope I didn't startle you."

"No, not at all."

"I'm much too excited to go up to my room. I was hoping to see you if you were still about."

"I was in the mood for a stroll."

"I can't thank you enough for the wonderful dinner."

"Jane and Salty deserve the credit. They were very enthusiastic about making it."

"Of course, it's not the dinner I want to talk about," Emily said quietly.

"I didn't think it was."

"We've made a decision."

Alice held her breath, not knowing what to expect. She was prepared to congratulate or commiserate, whichever was needed.

"We're going to get married."

"How wonderful!" Alice said with a broad smile. "I hope you'll both be very happy."

"I'm afraid it won't be a happily-ever-after union, not right away. We still have a great deal to work out."

Alice couldn't tell how Emily felt by the tone of her voice. Was she having regrets already? She didn't sound like a typical bride-to-be.

"Your job?"

"I'm going to keep it for a few more years. I don't feel ready to retire. You know how committed I am to bringing dental care to poverty-stricken areas of the world."

"Yes, and I couldn't admire you more."

"I am so blessed, a friend and a fiancé who both understand."

"Henry doesn't want you to retire?"

"No, he knows how important it is to me, and he isn't quite ready to give up all his business interests either."

"Will you live in Potterston?"

"Partly. Since I travel a lot, I can only live there off and on. And Henry is training one of his nephews to take over, so he'll stay in Chicago from time to time. It's not an ideal arrangement, but we couldn't face the alternative—not being together at all. We're going to have a quiet family wedding before the end of the summer."

"I think you're very wise," Alice said wistfully. "I hope you'll have many happy years together when you both decide to retire."

They talked awhile longer, then Emily excused herself to go to bed. Alice stayed on the porch, enjoying her favorite evening retreat and thinking about the decision her friends had made. She'd told Emily that it was a wise choice to be together as much as their separate lives allowed. Thinking of them, she always came back to her own separation from Mark. He'd been in her heart for a long time, and now he was back in her life. They tried to see each other whenever they could arrange it.

Would they both retire and be together full time? That time still seemed far off. She treasured his friendship and affection, but she was thankful for the opportunity she'd had to share her father's final years, for the career that fulfilled her deepest needs and especially for the faith that guided her in everything she did.

Chapter Sixteen

Jane wanted to dance through the parking lot crying "Praise the Lord." She could hardly resist telling her good news to strangers on the walkway.

This must be the way the lame had felt after Jesus healed them: relieved, grateful and joyous all at once.

Alice drove up with the car, saving her a rather long walk, but Jane felt as though she could make the trip from Potterston to Acorn Hill on foot.

"You're beaming from ear to ear," her sister said when Jane got into the car.

"I was hoping for good news, but the doctor said I healed as fast as a teenager. There are no more restrictions on what I can do. I can have my kitchen back."

"Just in time for Salty's recital at the inn."

"I'm going to fix him a send-off meal that will knock his socks off." She smiled broadly. "But don't say a word to him. He thinks we're only having a few friends over to hear him play."

"How will you manage to surprise him? He'll be cooking breakfast for the last time Friday, and he rarely leaves the inn before noon."

"I have it planned," Jane said with a grin.

"You couldn't have timed your recovery better. I thought Salty was staying until late June, but he's leaving nearly a week early, the day after his debut as a singer-pianist. He's been quite mysterious about the reason, but he did say that he has to go home to Ohio before his fishing trip. I have to admit I'm curious. He's become one of our team, almost one of the family, since he took over making the breakfasts."

"Well, he's in for some surprises Friday evening," Jane said with a grin.

"To begin with, he has no idea that we've invited nearly twenty people." Alice grinned mischievously. "I had Hope help me make a list of people he's met since being here. I even included Florence and her husband since Salty made quite an impression on her with his chocolate mousse."

"I hope you told him we're having a little buffet after he plays. I want him to be hungry."

"Yes, but it doesn't sound to me like you're planning cold cuts and potato salad from the grocery store."

"You know me better than that," Jane said, grinning at her big sister.

Louise smiled as she guided Salty through a rehearsal of the songs he would play for the first time to an audience Friday evening. He really wasn't half-bad. He'd accomplished his goal of learning to play a few World War I songs, and that seemed to satisfy his musical longings.

She had to give him credit for being tireless when it came to practicing. Nor was he her only success of late. Nina had proudly told Louise that she'd practiced nearly twenty minutes every school day for a week. This amounted to more time at the piano than she'd spent in all the preceding weeks.

"Now go ahead and sing along," Louise said, giving her blessing to his entire performance even though she would have preferred to erase "He's a Doughboy from Ohio" from her memory forever after hearing it so many times.

While he played, she thought about some good news Harvey Racklin had given her that morning. Thanks largely to Jane's persuasive powers, he'd agreed to be on a town committee to look into other ways of recycling. It wouldn't involve speechmaking on his part, and his expertise could certainly be of value. Jack O'Hara was going to serve too, and Jane couldn't be more enthusiastic about her role.

"You did that very well," Louise said automatically when Salty stopped playing.

"You're not just saying it to be nice?"

She smiled, still a little surprised that such a take-charge man had so many qualms about playing a few tunes. She was going to miss his presence at the inn, but not, to be truthful, his lessons.

"No, the recital will go as smoothly as a Salty-special breakfast."

Alice felt free as a bird Friday morning as she looked forward to a few days off work. Her first project was to continue where she'd left off in the garden. She'd finally finished planting the impatiens, but there would be room for other plants once she prepared some empty beds. If the weeds would stop growing for a few days, she might actually restore order to the untamed wilderness beside the inn.

She'd barely begun when Jane arrived beside her.

"You've made a good start," Jane said, "but you don't need to worry about the rest. As soon as my leg gets a little stronger, I'll take over. It's amazing how weak muscles can get when they're not used regularly."

"I don't mind, really. It's pleasant to be outdoors on a nice day like this."

"It does make you feel glad to be alive, doesn't it? I did want to remind you about shopping. I left a list in the top drawer of the desk. I didn't want Salty to see it in the kitchen. He mentioned getting a haircut this afternoon, so I'm fairly certain he won't be here. I don't want him to suspect anything."

Jane was having so much fun planning a surprise feast that Alice was more than willing to go to the grocery store. No doubt her sister was overdoing it, expecting her leg to be one hundred percent well right away, but there was no holding back Jane when she got an idea.

Jane had the time of her life that afternoon. With Salty safely out of the way and the groceries put away, she started creating in earnest. The main course for her buffet would be a giant bowl of tortellini, using a recipe she'd perfected. She garnished it with strips of yellow, red and green peppers, making it as colorful as it was tasty. Naturally, garlic bread was a must, but she didn't have time to make it herself. She settled for long, crunchy loaves from the bakery, splitting them and liberally buttering them so they were ready to heat.

Alice had swept, dusted and scrubbed the front porch, the best place to accommodate a large crowd in the summer. When guests were through with the folding chairs that they were setting up in the parlor for Salty's recital, those chairs could be moved outside.

The meal itself would be self-serve, arranged carefully on the dining-room table. Louise borrowed a stack of large plastic plates divided into sections from the church, and Alice convinced her that plastic tableware would be suitable for an outdoor party.

Jane wasn't concerned about the casual dishes and implements. Once people tasted her guacamole with crisp tortilla chips, they would know Chef Jane was back. As she chopped green chili peppers and onions for the dip, she thought about all the other luscious tidbits she planned to make. For a touch of class, she was making watercress sandwiches, a delicacy usually reserved for tea time, but one of her favorites.

Men always seemed to like her little franks in hot sauce, but what she most enjoyed making were pastry puffs. She would stuff half with sharp cheese and olives and the rest with her own mix of crabmeat, scallions, mayonnaise, lemon juice, egg whites and seasonings.

Jane hummed as she worked. It seemed like ages since she'd had this much fun. It wasn't about showing off for Salty. She was simply meant to cook.

Louise was nervous about Salty's debut. She tried to convince herself that it was silly to be concerned about the few songs he was playing. He knew them well. Their guests would be supportive, and everything would be fine. She'd arranged countless recitals for her piano students, some of them practically paralyzed with stage fright. Why was she worrying so much about a grown man?

She knew why, of course. Salty had become a friend during his time at the inn, and it would be a shame if his little concert wasn't a success. He badly wanted to honor his family members by performing for his veteran friends at home, and this should give him the confidence to do it.

Guests started to arrive, and he had yet to get there. It hadn't occurred to Louise that he might back out at the last minute, but it was unusual for him to be late. Sometimes it seemed that he arrived at the inn in the middle of the night to start particularly elaborate breakfasts.

Florence and her husband Ronald were among the early arrivals. Predictably, he was carrying a wooden-slatted picnic basket that Florence directed him to deliver to the kitchen. She rarely arrived at a social occasion without a sample of her cooking.

"You really didn't need to bring anything," Louise said.

"I wanted Mr. Loughry to sample my pickled beets and eggs," she said. "It's a recipe handed down from my grandmother. I'm sure he'll just love them."

"Well, thank you," Louise said, hoping there was a spot for them among the many good things Jane had prepared.

"Oh, I brought a crème brûlé too. It will have to go under the broiler just before it's served to melt the brown sugar into a nice shiny crust. I'm sure Jane won't mind."

"I suppose not," Louise said without conviction, certain that Jane didn't want the meal to turn into a potluck.

The parlor was filling up, and Louise was really worried when Hope showed up without her uncle.

"He said he'd meet me here," she said, looking especially smart with her short dark hair tinted a rich mahogany.

She'd dressed for the occasion in a mint green pantsuit with a lacy white blouse, but the festive effect was spoiled by her anxious expression.

"He's been acting peculiar lately. It's not like him to be secretive, and he's never late for anything."

Louise nodded. "I was beginning to wonder where—"

"Sorry I'm late," Salty said, rushing in the front door. "Glad you got here, Hope."

"Where have you been?" his niece asked.

"I had to take an important phone call from Ohio. I'm running late because I had an errand to do."

He was looking quite spiffy in a navy linen blazer with gold buttons and tailored gray trousers. He was wearing a white turtleneck shirt and penny loafers, a far cry from his usual kitchen attire.

"You have a tag on your sleeve," Hope whispered. "Is that what kept you, shopping for a jacket?"

"You caught me."

"I'll get scissors," Louise offered, hurrying into the office area and returning with them.

She gave them to Hope and watched as she carefully cut away the tag that had been sewn into the material near the cuff.

"Is everyone here?" Salty asked.

"If I counted right, they are."

"Then let's do this."

He certainly looked confident as he greeted people on his way to the piano. Louise stayed near the door, not wanting to intrude on his big moment. As she expected, he gave a short talk on his reasons for wanting to learn a few World War I songs, especially one his "doughboy" grandfather had written.

She held her breath as he began with "Over There." Either he had conquered his performance anxiety or he was very good at covering his nervousness. He played with confidence and enthusiasm, traits that sustained him during his next few numbers.

When he began singing and playing "He's a Doughboy from Ohio," her eyes grew moist. She always felt a surge of pride when a student did well, not for her sake as his or her teacher but because she knew what joy music could bring.

When he was done, the assembled friends applauded with genuine appreciation. His grandfather's song had more than made up for in sentiment what it lacked in musical excellence.

"Now I have something to tell you," Salty said, standing beside the piano. "Cooking at Grace Chapel Inn has been a life-changing experience. For a long time I've thought of opening my own little restaurant, but I always talked myself out of it. I was afraid I was too old or not enough of a businessman. Working with the Howard sisters has been a real eye-opener. They've taught me that the most important thing is to have a dream and the faith to carry it out. So I'm going back to Ohio before my fishing trip to sign the papers to buy a little place of my own."

Friends besieged him with congratulations and questions, wanting to know what kind of restaurant he had in mind.

"It's small, the lower floor of what used to be a private home. I'll live upstairs and it will only be open for dinner. You're all invited to the grand opening later in the summer."

"I don't know what your décor will be," Jane said, standing up to be heard over the buzz of voices, "but you might consider framing some sketches of a first-class chef. These are a thank-you for all you've done to help us. Our guests were fortunate to have you, and we're all very grateful."

Louise was almost as surprised as Salty when he opened a folder of drawings, each one showing him at work in the inn's kitchen. Jane had given them a comic twist without in any way seeming to mock him.

"I can't thank you enough," the big man said.

"Now it's time for dinner, a *Jane* special," she said laughing.

Alice shared her sister's regard for Salty and wished him well in his new endeavor. She did her best to be a gracious hostess, but part of her felt removed from the festive atmosphere. Maybe she'd reached an age where she regretted having friends leave. Emily's departure had made her a little melancholy, even though she and Henry were making a positive move in their lives.

Was her life static while everyone else's was in motion? Did she like her accustomed routine a little too much? Certainly the job switches of the past few weeks had thrown her a curve. She welcomed the return to business-as-usual just as much as Louise and especially Jane did, but she had a new appreciation for how much her sisters did to make the inn a success.

As their guests finished eating, she carried their plates to the kitchen and urged them to try the desserts, including Florence's contribution. Jane had provided a large sheet cake from the bakery with "Thank You, Salty," written in yellow letters on chocolate icing.

Jane had been wise to realize that not everything could be homemade this evening. Nevertheless, she'd probably overdone the time on her feet, but the smile never left her face. She was proud of her surprise banquet, but even prouder of the way she'd handled her time as an invalid.

"Alice, you need to come to the parlor," Louise said, poking her head into the kitchen.

"I was just going to put these leftovers in the fridge."

"Please just leave them. There are more important things to attend to."

The remaining guests were all on the porch, and she could hear Salty telling one of his navy tales. She was delighted that his farewell party had been so successful, but she was feeling weary.

"Go on," Louise urged.

Alice stepped into the parlor, dark except for one small lamp on a side table.

"I'm sorry I missed the party."

"Mark!" Alice couldn't have been more surprised.

"I didn't call because there was only a fifty-fifty chance I could get here tonight." He smiled broadly and gave her a big hug.

"Did you drive here from Philadelphia?"

"No, Pittsburgh. A friend at the zoo there asked me to consult on a problem they're having with a gorilla. I drove, thinking I'd surprise you on the way home. Fortunately I didn't have to stay as long as I thought, so here I am."

"Well, you've certainly surprised me. It's so good to see you."

"Louise told me that your substitute cook is leaving."

"Yes, he was a blessing while Jane's leg healed. He enjoyed cooking so much that he's going to open his own restaurant."

"Good for him. It's never too late for things—or people —you really care about."

"Would you like dinner? We have plenty left."

"No, I stopped for fast food on the way. How do you feel about a stroll in the moonlight?"

She slid her hand into his and led the way to the darkened garden at the side of the house.

Salty's Special Hot Clam Dip

½ cup butter
½ green pepper, minced
½ red pepper, minced
3 slices raw bacon, minced
1 medium onion, minced
1 teaspoon oregano
1 teaspoon parsley
Dash of Tabasco (hot pepper) sauce
2 6.5-ounce cans minced clams,
   reserve juice
1 teaspoon fresh lemon juice
½ cup Italian style bread crumbs
½ cup Parmesan cheese

Preheat oven to 350 degrees.

In a saucepan, cook butter, vegetables, bacon and seasoning until butter is melted. Spoon into baking dish.

In saucepan, simmer clams in lemon juice for fifteen minutes. Add clam juice as needed to keep mixture from getting dry. Blend clam mixture and bread crumbs with vegetable mixture in baking dish. Top with cheese and bake, uncovered, for twenty minutes.

About the Authors

Pam Hanson and Barbara Andrews are a daughter-mother writing team. They began working together in the early 1990s and have had twenty books published, including fifteen under the pseudonym Jennifer Drew.

Pam has taught reporting courses at West Virginia University and is now director of advising for the School of Journalism. She has presented writing workshops and has been involved in school and church activities. She lives with her husband, a professor, and their two sons in West Virginia, where she shares her home with her mother.

Previous to their partnership, Barbara had twenty-one novels published under her own name. She began her career writing Sunday-school stories and contributing to antiques publications. Currently she writes a column and articles about collectible postcards. For twenty years she has sponsored a mail postcard sale with all proceeds going to world hunger relief. She is the mother of four and the grandmother of seven.

A Note from the Editors

This original book was created by the Books and Inspirational Media Division of Guideposts, the world's leading inspirational publisher. Founded in 1945 by Dr. Norman Vincent Peale and his wife Ruth Stafford Peale, Guideposts helps people from all walks of life achieve their maximum personal and spiritual potential. Guideposts is committed to communicating positive, faith-filled principles for people everywhere to use in successful daily living.

Our publications include award-winning magazines such as *Guideposts*, *Angels on Earth* and *Positive Thinking*, best-selling books, and outreach services that demonstrate what can happen when faith and positive thinking are applied in day-to-day life.

For more information, visit us online at www.guideposts.org, call (800) 431-2344 or write Guideposts, 39 Seminary Hill Road, Carmel, New York 10512.